The *Writing* on the *Wall*

Souvenirs (1981)
Vermont River (1984)
The Man Who Loved Levittown (1985)
Hyannis Boat and Other Stories (1989)
Chekhov's Sister (1990)
Upland Stream (1991)
The Wisest Man in America (1995)
The Smithsonian Guide to Northern New England (1995)
Wherever That Great Heart May Be (1996)
North of Now (1998)
One River More (1998)
Small Mountains (2000)
Morning (2001)
This American River (2002)
A Century of November (2004)
Soccer Dad (2008)
Yellowstone Autumn (2009)
Hills Like White Hills (2009)
On Admiration (2010)

The *Writing* on the *Wall*

a novel

W. D. WETHERELL

ARCADE PUBLISHING · NEW YORK

Arcade Publishing books may be purchased in bulk at special discounts for sales promotion, corporate gifts, fund-raising, or educational purposes. Special editions can also be created to specifications. For details, contact the Special Sales Department, Arcade Publishing, 307 West 36th Street, 11th Floor, New York, NY 10018 or arcade@skyhorsepublishing.com.

Arcade Publishing® is a registered trademark of Skyhorse Publishing, Inc.®, a Delaware corporation.

Visit our website at www.arcadepub.com.

10 9 8 7 6 5 4 3 2 1

Library of Congress Cataloging-in-Publication Data is available on file.

ISBN: 978-1-61145-744-5

Printed in the United States of America

For Vasily Grossman

1905-1964

One

HAUNTED house, haunted woman, haunted country, haunted hills.

The match was perfect enough to make Vera smile for the first time that summer, the first time all year. In the dark, stooping, she reached for the key her sister had left under the lilac closest to the porch. The moon found it before her hand did, a nickel with a silvery nose. The house groaned when she applied it to the lock, but halfheartedly, as if it were tired of scaring, having done it for so many years. A creaking floorboard under her shoe, a film of cobweb against her cheek, the garlic smell of wood rot, and then she was in, there was nothing the house could do but accept her, saving its scarier tricks for later.

Jeannie had told her where the switch was for electricity, but she had neglected to write it down, and she was too exhausted to search. Exhausted from decisions, not big ones, nothing major, but the dozens of minor ones needed to get herself onto the plane in Denver, fly across the continent, drive north three hours from Boston and find her way here. She could sleep now—for the first time in months her heart sent permission to her head. She groped her way down the entrance hall, found moonlight again, used it to climb steep stairs to the bedrooms. The largest had a mattress on the floor, a light cotton blanket, and, centered on the pillow, Jeannie's welcoming little joke, a Snickers bar, the kind they always begged for as kids.

It was Jeannie's vacation house—their "shack" they were calling it, Tom's fixer-upper, a place they could go to when the pressures of the city got too great. Built in 1919, it had stood empty for the past sixteen years, taxes had gone unpaid, and the town was more than happy to sell it to them cheap. It was a forgotten kind of place, with no ski areas nearby to jack up prices, no pretty lakes, just a shallow stream running toward Canada which gave Tom visions of learning how to fish. Our "retreat" was the other term they used, without saying what they were retreating from, though Vera knew that the news of the world hit them hard. Terrorists wouldn't find them there, even if they took New York—and in the meantime, Tom could do his fishing, Jeannie could have a garden, and anyone who needed solace more than luxury was welcome to borrow it anytime they wanted.

"You can have it for two weeks," Jeannie told her when she called in June. "Three weeks. Right into August if that's what you need. We won't be able to get up there until after Paris and maybe not even then."

"I'd like to stay thirty days," Vera said. The precision was deliberate.

"There's no furniture yet. The yard is a jungle, I haven't touched the garden, and the vines look like they're gobbling the house. But it's interesting enough inside. Whoever built it must have had lots of birds-eye maple, because the floorboards, when we peeled the linoleum off, turned out to be gorgeous. Will Dan be coming?"

"No. Just me."

"He must be busy with his contracting again, good for him."

That was always Jeannie's way, to supply the white lie herself.

"I can't emphasize that enough," she said, when the silence went on a little too long. "How much work it all needs. The worst is the walls. They're plaster, original probably, but the wallpaper is straight from hell. The front rooms have something that resembles knotty pine, and whoever lived there in the Sixties put up something in the hall that looks like what wedding presents come wrapped in, this hideous white velvet with blood-colored veins. Stripping it off is going to be a major ordeal."

"Let me help."

"I'm sorry?"

"Let me do it."

It surprised her, the quick and powerful way the asking surged through her throat.

"Strip the wallpaper?"

"I'm terrible with tools, but I'm sure I can do it."

"It would take months."

"I'll work hard."

"Uh, Vera? It isn't easy."

"I know what you're thinking, that Dan is the carpenter and I'm just a teacher. But I'm not so klutzy I can't strip wallpaper."

"We've already talked to someone in town, an old French Canadian who does anything."

Surprising, how much she needed Jeannie's yes—enough so she brought out her most powerful argument, the one there was no refusing.

"It will do me good. To have something like that to focus on. It's what I need right now. I'll do a good job for you, I promise."

Jeannie was six years younger—she'd never had to beg her before. Quickly, almost too quickly, she reversed course and said yes. Why of course she could help, that would be wonderful. They could leave scrapers for her and putty knives and stripping solution and a stepladder and a big garbage can to put scraps in and rubber gloves and bandages in case she nicked herself and plenty of food and wine, and it would all be ready for her when she arrived, she could go right to work.

"You won't have to worry about a thing while you're there. Really—not a thing. It's grunt work though, really messy. How strong are your wrists?"

"Once I finish I can hang the new wallpaper. Have you picked any out?"

"After stripping? That's double the work."

"Downstairs then. You can hire your Frenchman to do upstairs."

"There's a website with old Victorian wallpaper and we found a soft peach color that complements the floor. Tom's doing the math on how much we need. But we'll order it and have it waiting with everything else."

"Thank you, Jeannie. Jeannie? Really, thank you."

"You know how much aggravation you'll be saving us? I'll send you directions. Basically, you drive north on the interstate, then fall off the map. Don't argue with me, but we insist on paying for your flight . . . That merger I told you about? It's back on again, so I have to be going."

She said goodbye abruptly, without asking about Cassie, and the absence of that kept Vera holding the phone for a long minute after she hung up. "She's well, thanks," she said to the mouthpiece. As well as can be expected. If she can stand thirty days then so can I.

Maybe that's what the chocolate on the pillow was for—an apology, a gesture of support. Certainly Jeannie had kept her promise about supplies. In the darkness, boxes and cartons made a maze she had to thread her way through before going upstairs. She glanced at the walls on the way up, traced her hand along the paper, but it was too dark to really see. Beside the candy was a penlight she used to find the bathroom; after undressing, she fell against the mattress as if she'd been pushed. Two layers of exhaustion worked on her, and the upper one, the one that came from the flight and long drive, was wonderfully smothering, the way it kept the bottom layer from having its way. She fell asleep quickly, dreamed of silly things, then, well before dawn, woke up to moonlight touching her face.

It burned, that was the odd thing, white as it was. She lay there until it touched her throat, then, restless, wrapped the cotton blanket around her shoulders and ventured carefully out into the hall. The walls weren't square and reliable, but slanted at unexpected angles, like baffles, keeping her from walking straight more than a few steps at a time. One turn brought her to a door with frosted glass in the upper panels. A closet, she decided, but when she opened it she came to a pool of moonlight so dense and liquid she stepped back in alarm.

There she found a little balcony, a platform big enough for a single chair, set above the porch just below. Someone must have built it to have a quiet spot where they could be alone over the hubbub of visitors, and this pleased her, to have discovered one of the house's secrets so quickly. The railing was wobbly and rotted, but it gave her enough confidence to take the three steps needed to peer down.

The ground mist rose into the moonlight, and toward the top were milky tongues that licked in toward the house. Back home the mist hardly ever rose above the sage, but here it seemed brewed from an enormous kettle, smelling of greenness and the lightest spice of fir. An enormous pine tree fronted the porch, but the fog hid its trunk and only the needles were visible, like pins holding the mist up. Jeannie had told her about the wild pea vines, and it was true, they climbed the porch and coiled around the railings, not eating the house so much as holding it ready to eat, shifting and turning it to just the right angle.

She could hear Tom's trout stream across the road, a purposeful rushing, and an owl, very distant, calling to a hoarser one that roosted much closer. She shivered as she listened, her new kind of shivering that had nothing to do with the damp. In March, she had been hurled out from the world by a single phone call and she wasn't down yet. Even on the flight east, after she had said goodbye to Dan, taken her seat, closed her eyes during takeoff. The plane didn't need to climb, she was already up there, and the entire flight had seemed a gradual downward slant, and yet never did she land. Even landing it didn't land. Even in Boston she wasn't down. And now here she was, climbing porches in the moonlight, on the way up again, her landing further off than ever.

She had spent the flight staring out the window, though her neighbors, absorbed in the movie, glanced sideways at her and frowned. It was an exceptionally clear day, the view should have been wonderful, and yet it was marred by something it took her most of the flight to understand. The land below looked tired and old—there was a graying agent in the air creating the effect of an exhausted giant sleeping with its mouth open; the lakes, its eyes, rheumy and clouded; the highway, its lips, crusted over with spittle; its hands, the valleys, listless and pale. The longer she stared, the more coma-like the effect seemed, and it made her angry, enough so she wanted to ring a bell or trip an alarm. "Wake up Detroit!" she wanted to shout, when the pilot mentioned it was under them. "Wake up Syracuse!" The pilot came back on to warn of turbulence, but the only thing shaking was her heart.

She turned around to take the house in, what she could see above the mist. Behind the porch the eaves rose at an angle so sharp it suggested a fierce-looking steeple. Under the edges drooped a trim of gingerbread so rotten it was impossible to understand why it hadn't dropped off. The single window had only one shutter, hanging out at a lopsided angle from the glass. Now, as she watched, it seemed aware of her presence, because, with no wind stirring, it creaked sideways on its hinges and smacked the window with a bang.

Excellent, she decided—for the second time that night she nearly smiled. Show me more of this, use your best tricks, frighten me out of my numbness, though to find numbness is exactly why I've come. Generations had lived and died there, the house reached back into time, so why shouldn't it be haunted, if only by rusty hinges, rotten joists, corroded pipes. Dan would have loved tackling these, he should have been the one to come. She could bring nothing to bear on the house except slow mindless work with her fingers, wrists, and arms, and yet maybe it was this that would make the house friendlier, coax it into her favor, calm all its fret.

She remained on the secret platform until she started shivering again, this time from cold. With it came exhaustion, and it was the deeper layer this time, the one that sleep could do nothing against. She went back inside to her mattress, pressed with her slipper until it slid away from the moonlight, and into the darkness let herself fall.

The difference in time zones worked in her favor—she slept much later than she did at home. The sun touched her face as the moon had, then moved across the floor to the nearest wall. When its light filled the room she got up, searched through her suitcase for a sweatshirt, tugged it down over her jeans. A midnight arrival was no way to start with the house. It needed to be approached in daylight, from a feeling of energy and strength. She went downstairs determined not to look at anything—she pressed her hands to her eyes like blinders—and then she was outside crossing the yard to the road, walking purposefully toward the sun.

It was a modern enough road, with two smooth lanes and absolutely no traffic. A hundred yards past the house a sign announced the village was three miles off, and beyond that on the crest of a little rise stood a smaller green sign that she fixed on as her goal. When I touch it I'll turn around.

The fog lifted through the trees, and the energy of this made the leaves toss sideways and dance. From the wet grass on either side of the road came a cinnamon scent from flowers that were new to her, with spiky blossoms only partially unfurled. There was an iron smell, too, from the mud in the gullies. Black-eyed Susans grew everywhere, with purple nettles and a tough-looking gorse. Flowers had always been her joy in life, wildflowers especially, so this, she decided, is where she would come during breaks in work.

The sign turned out to be farther away than it looked. She walked for another ten minutes, and what she found when she got there surprised her considerably.

You are standing on the 45th parallel it read, in dignified bronze script. *Halfway between the Equator and the North Pole.*

And this time she did smile—tentatively, surprised at herself, but finally letting it have its way. What amused her was to think that Jeannie's house lay a quarter mile closer to the Arctic than it did the tropics, and how this must explain the feeling, so strong when she arrived during the night, of sliding toward the planet's edge.

Irony was good for her—joined with the sunshine it sharpened her vision so she could see things plain. She turned and faced the direction of the house. It lay centered in a frame made by the steep hill behind it and the winding trout stream across the road—bigger than it seemed up close, boxier, uglier, squatting with a hasty, improvised look on its overgrown scrub of an acre, despite the fact it had endured there almost a century. The sharp eaves she had stood under during the night were plainly visible splitting the house in two, only now it seemed less like a steeple than a stubby guided missile ready to be launched from the metal gambrel of the roof. The siding, with the sun slanting against it, was a chocolate color fading toward leather, though many boards were in the process of dropping off. The chimneys, all three of them, tilted toward the roadside, and the one that sagged furthest pressed against a rusty TV antenna that was almost bent in half.

Lower, partly obscured by trees, was the porch, with screens blackened from mildew and totally opaque. The bay windows, bulging out on either side, seemed like the turrets of a battleship ready to blast anything approaching from the road. And that was what the house suggested, seen from the distance—great fragility and great strength, so she simultaneously felt surprise that it was there in the first place and certainty that it had been there forever.

"Quaint," Jeannie had called it, when all other adjectives failed. But it was the exact opposite of quaint.

Well beyond the house, just before the road curved out of sight, was a smaller, even shabbier, house, but it was too far away to tell if it was occupied. The hill directly behind Jeannie's was steep and rocky, cutting off any view toward the west, but the hills on the sides sloped more gently, so perhaps a sunset sometimes managed to sneak through. The fields around the house were open, but overgrown and swampy, and it was impossible to tell whether anyone cared after them. The forest started at the base of the hill, with thicker, more serious looking trees than the handful clustered around the house.

There was something Western in the landscape that surprised her, at least if you faded out the green. Not so much where she and Dan lived, but the high northern tier of Montana where they had gone on camping trips when Cassie was little. Jeannie had warned her that she would find the sky small and claustrophobic compared to what she was used to, but it wasn't that way at all, and to the northeast, across the stream, the hills uncoiled toward Canada, widening the horizon. In walking back to the house she noticed two parallel tracks worn deep into the meadow grass, reminding her of trails left by pioneers back on the prairies. Had wagon wheels cut them? She taught middle school science, not history, but she was reasonably sure the settlers who came here first had not used covered wagons.

She approached the house from the rear this time, pushing her way through the wild honeysuckle separating it from the meadow, scaring up some robins. There were shabby outbuildings, one filled with soggy black firewood, the other looking like a cross between a chicken coop and a barn. Swallow nests drooped in pendants from the rafters, but they were dry and sterile looking, fit for ghost birds, not live ones. Both buildings, in Jeannie's plans, were doomed to immediate demolition. A neglected stone wall marked the back of the property, now just a rock pile, nothing crafted, and the frost had long since toppled the upper boulders to the ground.

Other than these, there wasn't much to discover. Strands of barbed wire, tarry shingles blown off the roof, a mushy baseball. She stepped on something sharper than a rock, reached down, picked up a wedge-shaped spike scaled in rust. There was a path worn into the ground, with bleached-out grass, and it led right to the wall and not one step farther. Someone had once walked there, walked there often, but had never gone beyond the edge of the property, though the meadow behind it ran for another hundred yards before the forest. This saddened her—the sense of limits, of obedience, of self-imposed circumscription.

A fence led around toward the front. A picket fence, the slats gray and peeling, only not a picket fence, because the slats were pressed tight together. She struggled to remember the right term. Stockade? A stockade fence? Stockade as in fortress? Stockade as in prison? Again, as always now, she stepped upon the booby trap of words.

Only one tree grew in back, an enormous box elder. From the thickest branch hung a tire swing that must have dated from the 1940s, so old and petrified was its rubber. Vera, reaching, was surprised to have it actually sway. They had hung a tire swing like that for Cassie from the branch of their plum—the solid remembrance of pushing came into her arms, the moment she saw it. Cassie had been reluctant to climb on that first time, she had an only child's sense of prudence, but after that it became her favorite plaything for the whole of one summer, especially after sunset when she liked to swing back and forth kicking her legs out at the fireflies that flashed near her face.

"Higher Mommy!" she would yell—the little girl's classic plea. "Higher!"

Good memory? Terrible memory? She wasn't sure how to tell them apart anymore. Any walk she could find, any path, circled back to facing that.

In heading toward the back door, swerving sideways to get around a midden heap of rusty cans, she came upon a surprise. Poppies, tall ones, as brilliantly red as it was possible to imagine, their blossoms touching heads. They didn't grow wild, someone must have once planted them, and she felt comforted by this, the evidence of a loving human presence. And there was better than that, too. Behind the poppies was a cluster of blueberry bushes taller than her head, and around these, as a kind of barrier, thorny blackberries, with so much fruit the vines sagged. She ate some of the plumpest, filled her cupped hands with more, then and only then began to think of breakfast.

Stone steps led up to the kitchen. It was dark inside—past ten now, and the sun hadn't penetrated. A huge sink, zinc or cast iron, took up most of one wall, and past it was a gas range that must have been new in 1950. HOTPOINT read the raised lettering on front, though both t's were twisted. This was the one room in the house that wasn't wallpapered, but painted. The wainscoting, running up from the linoleum, looked greasy and dusty at the same time, and above it the walls were the color of raw liver. A piece of stovepipe stuck out from the ceiling like a fat cigar, but there was nothing under it other than a black scar on the linoleum where a woodstove had once rested. The room smelled of something she couldn't identify, but seemed part shoe polish, part charcoal, part skunk.

The only thing new was the refrigerator, which Jeannie had insisted on installing ahead of her visit. She had crammed it full of food, then piled even more on top. Half was the junk food they loved as girls, half was the organic that was Jeannie's new passion; Vera ended up having soy yogurt and a cellophane-wrapped cupcake for breakfast.

The bathroom was wedged in a corner behind flimsy walls. Vera, despite herself, knocked on the door before she went in— the door with heart-shaped openings cut in the panels to let heat flow through. The wallpaper inside had shiny red and green stripes like Christmas wrapping, but it was peeling and didn't look like it would be hard to strip. There was no tub or shower, which Jeannie had apologized for a dozen times over, but the hose worked out in the yard, and, if she felt adventurous, there was always the stream across the road for skinny-dipping or splashing.

The kitchen will be my base camp, Vera decided. I'll keep it neat and organized and not worry about the chaos everywhere else. Once breakfast was over she started upon an inspection tour of the rest of downstairs. And it was really very simple, at least as regards the basic layout.

The hall, the central hallway along which she had groped her way the night before, ran all the way from the kitchen to the front entrance. The stairs climbed one wall—they looked even steeper and narrower than they had in the dark, and most of the banister was missing. Three rooms opened off one side of the hall, two off the other side, each reached by its own door. On the west, front to back, was the main parlor, then a sewing room or den, then a smaller back parlor with boarded-up windows. On the east was a foyer with brass pegs, then a narrow closet, then a dining room that was the largest, most pleasant room in the house, with windows that ran all the way up from the floor and an old-fashioned ceiling fan that, upon her entrance, began stiffly spinning, as if showing off what it could do.

This was the geography, it was easy enough to understand, and on her second inspection she turned her attention to the details. The floors were as beautiful as Jeannie claimed—birds-eye maple that gleamed satin in the morning light. Transom windows were cut in the tops of the doors, and the one in the dining room was stained glass. The windows, old as they were, looked sturdy and formidable, with filigree trim around the sashes that matched the gingerbread outside.

These were the highlights, the little touches that had convinced Jeannie to buy. "Everything's horrid after that," she said on the phone, and she hadn't been exaggerating. Water stains on the ceilings expanded outwards in urine-colored rings. Plastic sheeting had been tacked to the doors to make up for gaps caused by the house's settling. A mirror framed by a toilet seat dominated the back parlor, along with a Mickey Mouse clock with the eyes gouged out. The curtains, what were left of them, hung like shrouds. Cobwebs lay thick in the corners, mice droppings littered the floor, and everything seemed possessed by the kind of cold that, having nothing to do with temperature, remained impervious to the sun.

Fireplaces would have helped, working fireplaces, but the one she found in the front parlor had collapsed into a shapeless mound. Lichen covered the stone—stalked cups, yellow nodules, rosettes of greenish-gray. The grate was still there, but in place of logs was a damp, cradle-shaped slurry where squirrels or chipmunks had once made their nests.

That left the wallpaper—the wallpaper she had been trying her best not to worry about before examining all the rest. Even with Jeannie's warning, it was hard to look at without shuddering. The rooms on the left of the hall were covered with a thick brown paper that was meant to imitate pine, complete with knots and grain, while the rooms on the right had a paper that was even thicker, a faded white velvet with red-pink squiggles that suggested frosting. It was hung badly—seams split apart from each other and hardened pimples of glue bubbled up in the cracks. Horizontal strips had been pasted on as patches above the radiators and baseboards, but the bottoms hadn't been trimmed, so in places the velvet dangled against the floor like a trollop's dirty skirt.

Jeannie had no information whatsoever about the former owners. The house had been empty for years before the town stepped in, squatters had apparently lived there before that, and like every abandoned home along the border it was said to have been a hiding place for drugs.

"So we're back in the Sixties, whoever papered it," Jeannie had said. "I picture her in—what were those awful slippers called? Mules? I picture her in purple mules, her hair up in curlers, reading women's magazines about the suburbs and how knotty pine was all the rage. That's half of her. The other half is someone who never had a fancy wedding and hung the velvet in revenge."

Vera wasn't sure Jeannie's profile was right. It wasn't a frustrated housewife she sensed, but someone brassier, bolder, a woman trying to break out. Maybe the walls had been falling apart, and the paper had been meant as a desperate cover-up or glue. Maybe she had known how ugly the paper was, hung it anyway as a mordant joke. Maybe a man had done the knotty pine, a woman the wedding cake, and after long hours of arguing the wallpaper represented a compromise, the house split in half.

She finished her inspection tour in the dining room. Approaching the window, noticing a two-inch piece of paper that curled away from the wall like a wilted leaf, she reached up and pulled as hard as she could on its edge. This happened fast, impulsively, and yet for a second her fingers imagined the strip peeling off all the way down to the bottom of the wall, lifting the strip next to it, then the one beside that, then the rest of the paper in the room, and then the other rooms, too—imagined, in her foolishness, that with one mighty, satisfying, god-like tug all the paper in the house would come off in her hand.

This is not what happened. The little rind of paper immediately ripped, taking a chunk of wall plaster with it, so, on that first touch, she had already damaged what she had pledged to protect.

Slower. She took a deep breath. Slower! She nodded to herself, then, frowning, to the wall. This couldn't be rushed, shouldn't be rushed, wouldn't be rushed. The task would determine the speed, she wouldn't dictate, and in any case, the slower the job the better for her.

As for supplies, the tools she needed to work with, Jeannie had gone a little nuts. The hardware store in town had been contacted, a delivery arranged, and everything that could possibly be of use in separating wallpaper from walls had been deposited in the front parlor in a massive pile. Stepladders, scrapers, putty knives, work gloves, buckets, sponges, mops and brooms, cotton rags, bristled brushes. This was low-tech stuff, easy to identify once she began picking through the pile, but there were also chemical things to use for stripping, powders packed in cartons and liquids in plastic jugs. In one box, once she tugged the padding out, was something that looked like a leaf-blower with a stubby snout. A steamer? She wasn't sure, but it looked dangerous and cranky; she closed the box and shoved it to the side.

There was more. A huge radio, the kind you might see at a construction site, armored in yellow rubber. A first-aid kit, with extra bandages. Yardsticks and rulers. A page torn from the local phone book with the names and numbers of contractors to call in case she needed help.

In a separate, neater pile, stacked on end like the pipes of an organ, were the rolls of wallpaper Jeannie had ordered online. There seemed to be a huge number of these—she wondered if Tom had made a mistake in his calculations. The wrapping made it hard to see what was inside, but the exposed edges revealed that it was indeed the soft peach color Jeannie had described.

She decided to start by stripping the foyer—the smallest room in the house. Finish there and she would have a minor victory to build on. After that she could tackle the front parlor, the room with the most sun, come out again to do the hall, zigzag to the sewing room and back parlor, then finish with the dining room.

No reason to delay. She went around opening the windows first, or at least trying to, their sashes were so old and swollen. The radio she propped up on the remains of the fireplace, fiddling with the dial until she came upon a station from Canada playing French music—easy listening, since she didn't understand a word. From the supply pile she selected a five-inch-wide putty knife, deciding she would start with the simplest tool and see how far she got with that.

A good part of the foyer was taken up by the front door. To its left, the wall was only one strip wide—a perfect place to start. The putty knife, with its fat grip, felt awkward in her hand, and she kept twisting it around trying to find the right balance. Dan was the artist with tools; she had always been helpless with them, and even the simple labs she did with her eighth-graders offered her all kinds of opportunities to mess up.

Did the wallpaper sense that? Did it know her weakness? In school, she made up for her clumsiness with humor, but the wallpaper would not be charmed by smiles or corny jokes.

It was the knotty pine paper—it looked as thick and unpeelable as wood—but there was a weak spot where the strip met the door frame and overlapped like a loose flap of skin. The one tip Dan had given her was to always start at the top near the ceiling and work down, so gravity helped with the peeling and the strips fell to the floor of their own weight. She reached—the edge was just wide enough she could get her fingers around it. As a girl, shopping with her mother, the butcher would lean over the counter and hand her a slice of bologna as a treat, and she would go off by herself to the produce section and carefully peel off the rind. Pulling the first strip of paper was like that, easy and satisfying, though it was disappointing that only the overlapped edge came off, not the paper that was glued.

She went to fetch the stepladder, picked a spot where the wall met the ceiling in a shallow crevice. The putty knife was sharp—she held it edgewise and sawed until there was a spot where the blade could gain purchase and lift. She did this gently, but at an angle that was far too acute, so the blade dug into the plaster. The trick seemed to be holding it at a flatter angle to the wall, more like a spatula than a knife. By doing so, she was able to get under the edge and pry, but, after a second's worth of tension, only a nickel-sized piece of paper broke away. She watched it flutter down past the ladder to the floor, feeling both triumph and despair.

The good news was that the sliver of paper, in dropping, had created a slightly larger edge, a slightly larger vulnerability. She flattened the scraper to the plaster, twisted her wrist sideways as far as it would go, pushed to the left, then, when there was enough tension against the blade, lifted firmly outward. This time a bigger piece came off, a quarter instead of a nickel, but again she had gouged the plaster and she was still very far from getting the knack.

"It's either going to be easy or fucking impossible," Dan told her, and it was obvious now that it wasn't going to be easy. Whoever had originally glued the paper had spread it on thick, and the decades had made it even tougher, more resin-like, so the paper clung to the wall for dear life. By concentrating, sawing to get an edge, scraping to get underneath, using her fingernails, she could lift off nickels and sometimes quarters and occasionally a silver dollar, but the pieces fell off individually, they couldn't persuade adjoining pieces to follow them, let alone entire strips.

The top third she did on the ladder, the middle standing close to the wall, the bottom third on her knees. She cut her wrist, dust watered up her eyes, and the muscles in her forearms felt tight as cord. Still, she had done it, her first strip—its woodsy looking duff lay at her feet. Thirty minutes for one narrow strip. To do the rest of the house would take thirty years.

But just having that one strip off seemed a huge improvement—the plaster was a soft linen color, and having it exposed was like adding a strip of daylight to the gloom. The next strip she tackled, on the left side of the door, was even harder, but she tried not to take it personally—the maddeningly stubborn malevolence of certain impossibly hateful bits. She would be edging the scraper along, making real progress, getting under an inch, an inch and a half, even two inches, when suddenly the blade would skip off a hardened bubble of glue or an unusually tough corner, and nothing would come off, so instead of scraping she would have to use the putty knife as a chisel. Even then some spots resisted. The parts of the paper that were meant to resemble knots turned out to be knotty, as if whoever had manufactured the paper had stirred in bark, and she quickly grew to hate these petrified dark spots most of all.

Even with this she managed to clear the strip off in twenty-three minutes, improvement enough for a ludicrous moment of pride. She noticed something this time she had missed earlier—traces of old wallpaper that the last person to strip the walls, the Sixties woman responsible for the knotty pine, hadn't completely scraped off. Small as these pieces were, they were layered three thick, and wondering about them made her feel like an archeologist. The bottom layer was surely the original wallpaper pasted on in 1919 when the house was new. Whoever had bought the house next, instead of scraping off the original wallpaper, had just papered over it, and then some years later, a new owner, equally lazy, had pasted over that, so the walls must have been looking thick and lumpy by the time the Sixties owner—who was beginning to seem like a real hero to her—took the bull by the horns and scraped off everything down to bare plaster, or at least everything but these leftover, layered pieces.

It took extra effort, scraping these off. The upper layer, the one that must have gone on in the Forties, was a drab green color, and the layer under that, probably from the Thirties, was a cheap Depression mustard, but the one beneath that, the original 1919 paper, was a faded, feminine and very delicate peach color not all that different than what Jeannie had picked out for her restoration. There wasn't much left of this, just those bottommost traces, but it was enough to convince her that, go back far enough, someone had loved the house after all. Certainly, of the four papers ever hung there, it clung tightest, most faithfully to the walls.

She worked for another hour, this time on the wall opposite the door, then, with her arms aching, decided it was time to allow herself a break. Jeannie had stocked the refrigerator with vitamin waters, organic lemonade and soy chocolate milk, but she ignored these and boiled tea water on the stove. She took the mug back to the parlor, cleared a spot amid the supplies, rummaged until she found the box she was looking for, sat herself down to read.

Even with the improvement it was going to take forever to strip the walls. In the box was a powdered remover you mixed with water and applied to the wallpaper with rags or a sponge. The directions said to begin by "scoring" the paper, which she was reasonably sure meant scratching x's that would allow the solution to penetrate. It must have been extraordinarily strong stuff, because the directions suggested wearing rubber gloves during application and covering your eyes. There were darker warnings below that—birth defects, in using this product, were known to occur, at least in California.

Any combination of words and phrases could trip her up now, it didn't take something as stark as "birth defects." And what kind of defects were they talking about anyway? Physical defects? Mental defects? Moral defects? There were more than one kind, why didn't they spell them out? Use this product and your baby might be born without arms. Use this product and your son might develop Asperger's. Use this product, use it repeatedly, and your daughter might grow up not knowing right from wrong.

She could blame herself for a lot of things, but not that— nineteen years ago she had not been stripping wallpaper with poison powders. Even now she was reluctant to use it. She went back out to the kitchen, filled a bucket, came back, shook some powder in, sloshed it around with a rag, then, after making a small x with her putty knife, wiped the slurry white of it across a small section of foyer wall. The directions said to wait fifteen minutes before scraping, so she worked along the ceiling first, then climbed back down the ladder to see if the stuff actually helped.

It did and it didn't. The treated paper was much softer, easier to scrape, only the smell was horrible, enough to make her gag. Dan had warned her that in the old days they used horsehair in plaster, and wetting it would bring out the smell—only there seemed to be goat hair mixed in, too, goat droppings, goat piss. The strips that came off were a soggy mess that immediately stuck to the floor, so she would end up having to scrape that, too, doubling the work.

No shortcuts then—every inch she would peel by hand. She worked the rest of the afternoon, determined to finish the foyer before quitting, though it was late into the evening before the final strip came off. The scraps formed a dusty pyramid she kicked toward the door, too tired to do anything more. Her fingers and wrists were numb—her knuckles looked worked on by a grater. She went outside to the yard, found the hose Jeannie had told her about, took off her clothes, turned the faucet on full strength, then, bracing herself for the cold, blasted off the papery bits caught in her hair.

Once she toweled off and dressed again, she walked back through the yard to the old stone wall. She was too late for the sunset—there wasn't much left now except a purple-edged cloud. A cloud like that back in the Rockies would mean a thunderstorm—and soon, but here the air seemed too soft to support anything that flashy. To the south toward the village arced a pinkish seam that may have come from streetlights, but back the other way, toward the neighboring house and Canada, there were no lights showing whatsoever.

She fixed hot dogs and corn muffins for dinner. The electricity worked now, but she found a kerosene lantern in the pantry and it felt more appropriate to use that. She busied herself upstairs arranging her clothes on the bedroom floor in some semblance of order, then slid the mattress farther away from the window so the moonlight wouldn't wake her again. The layout of the rooms upstairs was even simpler than downstairs—two bedrooms and a small bathroom grouped around the lopsided craziness of the hall.

She took the lamp, explored the bedroom next to hers, and immediately came upon another of the house's secrets. There was a closet in the middle of the wall, and when she opened it, stuck in the lamp, she could see it ran the entire length of the house. She wasn't sure, the light wasn't quite strong enough, but it seemed to end in a small, Alice-in-Wonderland-type hole. Where could it lead? It would open out from the house, not back into the hall. Was there a shed there? Had there once been an attached barn? Why would anyone use a closet to exit the house? Her opening the door must have disturbed the air flow, because a soft panting sound started up at the tunnel's far end. "Be still!" she commanded, in her best teacher's voice, and immediately the sound stopped.

As tired as she was, the core knot of restlessness had its way with her—she woke up at midnight just as she had the first night. Once again, she went out onto the balcony over the porch. Again the shutter began flapping, but she expected that now, it was probably caused by her weight on the planks. With less mist, the moonlight was purer, and the house threw out shadows so fang-like and vicious they looked make-believe.

The house enjoyed its distortions, but there was one that was genuine. Little motes of chartreuse danced up and down over the lawn, none of them managing to make it higher than the porch, but startling her all the same. Fireflies—it was late in the season for them—and they seemed bigger than the ones at home and many degrees brighter.

She had an impulse to duck, watching them. It was odd, they were nowhere near her head, but she felt that she must immediately duck. One summer when Cassie was seven the fireflies had been unusually thick, and they brought her outside to show her how to capture them in a jar. Cassie didn't want to do this—she already hated any kind of cruelty to animals, even though they promised to immediately release them. Instead, she ran inside to her room, came back out again holding something hidden behind her back. When she had their attention, she brought it out, her tremendous surprise.

A lite stick, a chemical lite stick she had been given on Halloween and had kept hidden in her bedroom ever since. She shook it back and forth now the way the instructions said, and when the light started glowing it was exactly the same chartreuse color as the fireflies. She held it out to them and waved it back and forth like she was conducting their dance, laughing in joy.

The memory of Cassie's lite stick came back to Vera so vividly it was almost staggering—again, she felt thankful for the railing. But it was cold and she felt more than dizziness centered in her stomach, so she wanted to lean over and clutch herself, clutch herself hard. She felt tears forming close to the surface ready to come spilling out—useless tears, sentimental tears, tears that weren't deep enough to help. She didn't let herself bend to them— she made the hard little grimace that was enough to hold them in. Later she could cry. Later when the tears came deeper. Later when they could do her some good.

She changed strategy in the morning. With the foyer stripped, she had planned to start on the front parlor, but on her way there, walking down the hall, she decided to test the velvet wallpaper with a scraper to see if it would come off any easier than the knotty pine. Once she got going, it was impossible to stop, even though the velvet turned out to be a much tougher proposition. With the knotty pine paper, she could sometimes manage to scrape off four- or five-inch pieces and occasionally be rewarded with a foot-long peel. With the velvet, she was lucky to pry off an inch at a time, and it was all about niggling, chipping, trying not to curse.

She put the radio on—the Quebec station with its soft *j'adores* and *je t'aimes*. After a while, she listened to the walls more than to the music, the coaxing sounds made by her scraper. Tinny scratch-es meant a stubborn spot; sandy whiskings meant a piece that could be lifted and peeled. With the foyer, she had worked from top to bottom, but here in the hall it was easier just to start in the middle and follow the path of least resistance. She began to think of the cleared areas as maps—here a map of Italy, here a map of Spain. I'll take a break and come back and expand Italy, she told herself. After lunch I'll double Spain.

She had thought her attitude might be more relaxed on the second day, but she had to work hard on not regarding the wallpaper as her enemy. To balance this, the walls became increasingly her friends. They were smooth underneath the paper and remarkably unblemished—their linen color was clean and inviting, of an era before cheap ugliness was born. Stripping the paper hurt her fingers, nails, and wrists, but the walls didn't hurt at all, not by stinging, not by cutting, not by reminding. They were beautifully blank in that respect, therapeutically blank. They were doing exactly what she hoped.

Of course the walls weren't perfect in that respect. Just because they carried no memories didn't mean memories didn't come. At the worst moments, when her arms started aching and her forehead dripped sweat, she began wishing she had someone to help her, and that naturally led her to think about Cassie who was so good at any kind of work requiring delicacy and patience. Organization, too—she was a great organizer, with assembly lines her specialty. Baking cookies with the Girl Scouts? An assembly line, assigning each of her friends a different task. Puppies needing their baths? Mom to dip, Dan to lather, Cassie to rinse and dry, the squirming puppies passed hand to hand until they were immaculate.

Cassie would be a pro at wallpapering. During high school she had helped Dan in the summers—she was on her way to becoming a skilled carpenter if she managed to stay interested. In their town, very early, the divide became apparent between young people who would go on to college and those who would work as hairdressers and mechanics. Cassie had friends in both groups, which was hard; she was always trying to find a middle way between futures, and this led her to considering the military. She was too restless to sit in college for four years, at least right away, and she was too ambitious to join the other girls who had already dropped out.

Two years in the National Guard, she decided—they had gone on a picnic and she was very solemn about breaking the news.

Dan had been more surprised than she had been—he barely managed to control his grimace. "We're very proud," he mumbled.

Cassie smiled, or tried to. "I'll fight forest fires and help with floods," she said. "I'll do my two years, and then since I love animals I'll apply to veterinary school at State."

She wasn't the first in the family to be a soldier. Dan's father fought on Okinawa, then entered Hiroshima three days after the bombing; he and Cassie, in his last years, had grown very close. Her dad, Cassie's other grandfather, was drafted in the Fifties and sent to Germany. Elvis Presley was in his company, and bought all the men poodles they could give to their girlfriends. That was how his two years had gone—Lowenbrau, frauleins, and fun. He took Russian lessons, but only so he could say the words "I surrender" to the first Soviet soldier he encountered if invasion ever came.

A joke, his army years. And now, in his granddaughter, the joke had turned serious.

That was Cassie—organized and efficient. Dan, on the other hand, would be no help whatsoever when it came to stripping. He would storm in, roll his sleeves up, start hacking away at the paper, anxious to get it over with as fast as possible. Leaky pipes, sagging joists, flapping shutters—those were the kinds of repairs he enjoyed making. "I need a man's job," he would say, making sure he winked. And she wondered if maybe he was onto something there. She knew it was wrong to even think in those terms anymore, but there was something feminine about stripping wallpaper that appealed to her greatly. Not feminine in a girly-girly sense, but something deeper, so she too found what her friends said they found in taking up knitting, mending, or canning. Solace, or something close to it. Being in touch with the old ways and finding in them peace.

I have wallpaper for comfort, she told herself. Dan has lies.

Harsh of her, unfair, but it's how she thought of things now. One second she would be concentrating on the latest, most stubborn piece of wallpaper, the boot of Italy or the north half of Britain, scraping away as if she didn't have any other concern in life but that—concentrating, squinting, probing—and then suddenly the paper would lift off, and in the brief vacuum before she started on the next piece the thought would jump out at her seemingly from nowhere. My husband is held captive by lies.

People had different ways to cope with pain, she understood that as well as anyone, and if Dan had decided to pop lies to get him through the months leading up to the trial, then fine, she almost envied him, and in any case they wouldn't hold him forever, he was too smart for that, he had too much sense. For now, it helped him, words like "duty," and "honor" and "patriotism," and the gruffly unctuous types who swarmed around him with those and similar words always on their lips.

Thinking of him made her feel guilty—she had kept her cell phone off ever since she arrived, and there was no other way he or Jeannie could contact her. Postcards and letters of course, the old ways, and she promised herself to write some when she had time. Her goal was to finish the white velvet half of the hall before the day was over, and by working straight through until dusk she managed everything but a final strip. She gathered up the scraps in her arms, carried them outside to the backyard, started a fire. Each scrap still held a residue of glue, so they burned very fast, and by the time she carried out another armload the first batch was already reduced to ashes.

It was clear out, less humid. Crickets were noisy in the warmth, frogs croaked out in the meadow, but instead of the owls she had heard the first two nights came the warbly keen of coyotes.

She walked around to the front of the house to hear better— in the darkness, she almost bumped into the car, the rental car she had parked there the first night and then forgotten. Jeannie had told her about a general store in the village, a library with free Internet, but she was too absorbed in her work to break away, and the thought of meeting anyone, engaging in small talk, did not appeal to her either.

"Maybe I'll take a break when I'm halfway done," she had told Jeannie on the phone when they first made plans. "I'll drive to some museums or state parks."

Even over the phone she could see Jeannie's eyebrows shoot up. "Museums? Parks? Up there? You've got to be kidding!"

There was enough beauty right there if she wanted it. Jeannie had stocked the pantry with another of her affectionate jokes— the cheap sangria they had pretended to like when they were teenagers. She poured some in her tea mug and brought it outside, laying down on the weeds near the dying remnants of the fire, her head propped against a rusty lawn chair that must have been new in 1960. By staring straight overhead she could make out the summer triangle: Vega, Altair and Cygnet the Swan, its neck pointing north, its wings flapping open toward lesser, fainter stars she didn't have names for. They shone brighter than they did at home, which surprised her, since she always pictured Eastern skies lit garishly by shopping plazas and malls.

There were no malls here—the stars, after her second mug of wine, seemed close enough to stroke. She taught an astronomy section in science, hosting star parties with a telescope so her students could take turns peering up at Saturn or Mars. She wondered where those boys and girls were now, the eighth graders she had last year, the seventh graders who would have her in the fall. It was only eight o'clock back home, she could picture them wrapped in towels at swimming pools or sitting on the grass in the twilight watching their dads play softball, talking among themselves about the coming year.

You having Mrs. Savino next year for science? She's nice, you'll really like her, as long as you do your work. You having Mrs. Savino next year for science? She so used to be nice, but she's grumpy all the time now. You having Mrs. Savino next year for science? It was weird, really weird, but last year in fourth period she suddenly turned toward the blackboard, covered her face in her hands, and began like almost to sob.

Two

THE third day was much the same, as was the fourth and fifth, and her great discovery didn't come until Saturday, with the very first piece she stripped from the wall.

She had finished both sides of the hall and was ready to shift her attention to the front parlor. To the left of the window was the obvious place to start—a protruding edge where two seams overlapped right there at face level. She had learned to look for these vulnerabilities, and so, not thinking much about it, she slid her putty knife under the seam, wedged further, then lifted.

The piece came off easily enough, though it was disappointingly small. On the wall beneath it was something she thought at first was an insect, a petrified spider. She started scraping, then realized the spot didn't protrude but was flush with the plaster. It looked like a stain, a calcified black stain, taking on a crescent shape before disappearing under paper she hadn't yet scraped off.

Careful Vera, she told herself, though she wasn't sure what she was responding to or why caution came over her so fast. She put her face up close to the wall and squinted, making sure she only got paper and didn't scratch the plaster underneath. More of the stain slowly became visible, enough so she finally understood what it was. The letter *c* written in black ink, india ink, with a precision and gracefulness that could only be from a different era.

An initial? It was lower case, it couldn't be meant for initials. It was partly hidden under a three-layer fragment—under, which meant it had to have been left there by whoever first papered the walls back in 1919. The ink was faded the same way the bottom layer of paper was, so it was reasonable to assume it had been applied just before the wallpaper and they had aged through the decades together.

She rummaged through the supplies for a smaller putty knife that would work more delicately. To the right of the *c* was an *r* and an *e*. She put her cheek so tight to the wall that her vision couldn't make out what came next, and only after uncovering the next five letters did she bring her head back and read.

credence

It was like someone's voice spoke the word out loud—in the silence, she took the surprise of it straight into her heart. An old-fashioned word, one she had to think about for a moment before understanding. *Credence.* The last *e* wasn't quite cleared yet; in scraping off its final loop, she came upon a period, so it was obvious, if she was going to uncover the entire sentence, she had to work back to the left.

Mrs. Hodgson said he asked about me but I gave this no credence.

The handwriting was beautifully proportioned, flowing along with perfect naturalness, though it must have been wearying to hold a pen that high. The script part, the little decorations, flourishes and curls, was particularly graceful, and gave the impression a breeze was blowing the sentence across the wall. The *o's* were round and open, almost prissy, but the *t* and *i's* looked rebellious, the cross bars and dots drifting well to the right of where they should be. The first letter in *Hodgson* was wonderfully bold and exaggerated; Vera, staring at it, realized she had forgotten what a capital *H* in script even looked like.

It was already ten now, time for her tea break, and she forced herself to go ahead with this. When she came back to the parlor, stared up again at the wall, she experienced a moment of very intense shyness, as if there were a person in the room after all, and, having spoken those first words to her, it was now her turn to say something back.

She stepped back to appraise the wall from a distance. It was obvious that anyone writing on the wall would begin on the top left corner. They would have plenty of room that way, the window was well to the right, and the wide expanse of plaster would have suggested a blank sheet of paper or the empty page of a book. If that was the case, if her hunch was correct, then the sentence she uncovered would have occurred well down from the start. To expose the rest meant sliding the ladder over, putting it tight against the wall, reaching up as high as she could.

In the top left corner was wedged the name *Alan,* which she uncovered all at once, the wallpaper being friendlier there, more supple. The rest of the sentence was easy, too, as was the line below that, then the line below that—lines she didn't let herself read until she had six of them exposed.

Alan has gone to the city with his lumber and planks. For five or six days he tells me. When you return I will have the paper on I promised when I kissed him goodbye. I had not kissed him in a long time and it is a long time since I have been alone. He is different than he used to be. Because of what he did? Because of what he did not do, could not do? He seemed surprised by my kiss. He put his hands on my shoulders and turned me to the light, stared down hard at me, then, just before he let go, nodded and I think maybe sobbed.

Vera read this twice, three times, running her nails along the letters trying to scratch off the stubborn specks of paper that still adhered. Her reactions came so fast they were hard to separate. The feeling of the past coming alive beneath her hands—prying open a coffin couldn't have given her the sensation in such strength—plus the impression that light had flooded into the room, a radiance that had been captured and released from a shroud. Who had written this, when, how, why? The questions jumped out at her all at once, but even faster came the realization that the only way to find answers was to uncover even more.

She understood one thing immediately—she could not be the first person to read this. There was the top layer of knotty pine paper, the two nondescript layers beneath that or at least the flecked remains of that paper, then, on the bottom, the faded bits of papery peach that must have been original. That was the chronology, and all she had to do to understand it was reverse it, starting back when the house was new. Blank wall, words written on wall, paper pasted over words. New owners, lazy owners, paper pasted over paper. New owners, lazier owners, paper pasted over paper over paper. New owner, energetic owner, strip top layer, strip middle layer, strip bottom layer, uncover words, read words, cover them up again with the ugly knotty pine.

The next strip she peeled was nearly her record when it came to length, but there was nothing beneath it except blank plaster, which disappointed her greatly. So it was just a brief, random message after all, little more than a doodle, written there on a whim. But she was wrong on this. Once she cleared another eight inches the writing surfaced again—the writer, whoever she was, enjoyed beginning her paragraphs with deep indentations.

I was born on Christmas day in 1903 during the famous blizzard. I do not know the name of my father but Mrs. Hodgson once told me she thought he might be Selah Tompkins who worked with horses in the woods and was reckless and let a sled ride over him as everyone always knew it would. Mrs. H. sometimes seemed about to tell me who my mother was but always shook her head at the last moment. At the home there were four of us named Elizabeth so to avoid confusion one stayed Elizabeth, one became Liza, one became Lizzy, and I became Beth. Liza grew up and went down to the mills, Lizzy went to work for a preacher's wife out in Indiana and I was the only one who stayed here. Elizabeth, who got to keep her name, ran away to Boston which meant running away to be bad.

Reading as she scraped made Vera dizzy—her close vision blurred the letters up, smeared their blackness, giving her the disorienting sense they were an inky black pool and she was about to fall in. She went for her glasses, but they made it worse. The only way to proceed was to clear large sections off at a time, then and only then let herself read. Stripping would give her a goal, a focus— reading would be her break, her reward.

She worked an hour, got the first two strips off, went out to the kitchen to make herself a sandwich, came back and cleared three strips more. The words had waited patiently under the paper all those years, but now that they were exposed to light they seemed actively reaching out to her, demanding to be understood. Sensing this made her hurry and hurry made her clumsy. She scraped too hard—the blade skipped up and cut her finger, so her blood made a film over the writing which wiping only blended in deeper. She thought about using the stripping solution again or even trying the steamer, but worried they would be too harsh, too erasive.

A thunderstorm came up in the afternoon, the hills concentrating the noise and doubling it, until the house shook with each clap. The rain brought the dark on early, forcing her to stop. By then, she had one wall entirely cleared. She was going to put the lights on to read, but then discovered the power had gone off, forcing her to search for the kerosene lamp.

The words must have been written in such a light—if anything, the softness made the ink stand out more vividly, with more force. She set the lamp down on the top step of the ladder, and by moving it closer to the wall or back again she could illumine different paragraphs in a well-defined arc. Seen from a distance, the lines looked like a book, they were so neat and regular, and she realized that this had probably been Beth's intention, to make it all resemble a book. Lines extended across the wall, stopped at the same right margin, then started up again precisely a half inch below, and so on in the same pattern all the way from the ceiling to the floor—and then over again, only this time one full strip over to the right. Between the regularity and neatness it was amazing how many lines fit in.

They say I was a quiet child except when I had a friend and then I would pour my heart out. But I think there were never many friends. I remember when I was six, Independence Day came and they sent Mounties down from Canada in their red uniforms to march in the parade. I remember skating on the pond in our shoes since we had no skates. I remember dandelion necklaces we pretended were gold. Not much else beside this. They taught us always to sit with our hands folded, whether it was in class or at dinner or saying our prayers, and I knew even then what they really wanted us to do was hold in our thoughts, keep them small and tidy and confined. I could not do this very well. My thoughts made my hands tremble. Someone was always shouting "Don't fidget!" at me and the more they yelled the more my hands wanted to explode.

It was easier once I learned to read, things grew bigger. Later, Peter Sass teased me about this. "Did you starve in your orphanage?" he asked, with his amused little look that he never allowed to become harder. "Orphans are supposed to starve. Why, just think of Oliver Twist!"

I almost starved I felt like saying. But it had nothing to do with food.

Our books were Sleepy Hollow, Man Without a Country, Message to Garcia, The Queen of Sheba and Ned Buntline. That

was for the boys. For girls they had Wide Wide World and
Quechee. They were about orphans and how they married rich
men and we read them over and over again because they were the
only books that told us how to act as orphans. I read faster than
any of the girls or even the boys, but this only made everyone mad
at me, they said I was becoming capricious, taking on airs. How
can books do anything bad to you? I wanted to ask. It was an important question because inside them is where I lived.

I was eleven when I left. The Hodgsons bid lowest for me and
if you bid lowest the state had to hand you over. I was lucky since
they were both very kind. They never had children of their own
which was a pity. I helped Mrs. H. in the kitchen and caring for
the house. She was so cheerful that this was easy for me, though
the work could be hard. I helped Mr. Hodgson, too, times when
he had trouble getting hired men. Their farm was the highest in
town, all the other hill farms had been abandoned, but he always
swore he would be last to give up. I liked helping him mend walls,
since he still used oxen and he let me slap their flanks and shout
at them to get moving. He laughed when they just looked at me
and refused to budge, as if saying "Who is this pigtailed little girl
and why is she so bothered?"

I loved seeing things from the distance. When we finished
work I would stick my arms out and balance my way along the
stone wall past the briars to the highest part. In July where the hills
unfolded was like a huge green comforter rolling away toward
Canada, with a giant hand underneath plumping it out. Looking
at this blew my smallness away and I vowed never to let it back.

I turned fifteen on Christmas the year the war commenced
over in France. Mrs. H. wanted to have a talk but she knew it

would distress me so she waited until the following week. It was snowing and we had stopped sewing to watch a deer try to hop her way through the drifted field.

"Well," Mrs. H. said when we both sat down. "You're grown now and that means we need to be looking after your future. There are lots of things you could be doing and it's up to you which one to choose. Not right away. Why you can stay with us as long as you want. But presently."

I could see it was hard for her, so I nodded, tried my best to smile.

"You could go down and work in the mills, they treat their girls very well now, it's not like it used to be."

She said this calmly but could not help frowning.

"You could go out west like so many girls, Iowa or even Montana, they have special trains, and we would arrange for you to work for a respectable family."

She said this even more calmly but once again frowned.

"Or for that matter you could stay right here and get married. Not right away of course. In time. There are so few young men left but we would find one."

She made her voice all bright, but once again her frown betrayed her. I did not give her an answer, because there was one thing I dreaded and finally had to ask.

"What about school? Vacation is over tomorrow and I want to go back."

She looked at me and I read her look and turned away from it, we both turned away, since we knew how she had to answer and it was the first time she ever caused me pain.

"School is over for you, Beth. Why it would be high school and you know we can't afford to board you out. You're the smartest pupil in class, they always tell us that, and we know how much you love reading. I was talking to the principal and he says you can come back in June and deliver the commencement and you're the first girl they ever asked."

I tried keeping up. The library in town was six miles through the snow, but Mrs. H. would invent errands for me, parcels she wanted dropped at the various farms, since she knew they would give me something warm to drink and let me dry off by their fire. I tried keeping up in arithmetic and history but I could only carry so many books and there was so much I wanted to read just for pleasure. I had never read poetry before but now I read all I could. They had Ella Wheeler Wilcox, Sara Teasdale and Robert Service, though the librarian did not want me to read him since there was swearing in his poems. "Were you ever out in the Great Alone?" one of his best ones began and I kept saying that to myself over and over during the long walk back to the farm.

They had better than that. Helen Hunt Jackson's Ramona I read again and again. Elizabeth Barrett Browning I read because we shared first names, then because I loved her books more than anyone's. Aurora Leigh was about a girl growing up in Florence and marrying her cousin Romney who does not want her to be a poet since women do not have the brains and courage needed to write poetry. She leaves him and moves to London where I liked the story best, Aurora living by herself writing poetry.

No one had checked this out in years. None of the books I read had been checked out in years. It was as if books were deliberately left in the library to rot while everyone went off to the moving pictures and it was only me in the world who still cared for them. Sometimes when I took them off the shelves I imagined them sighing in happiness and relief, finding someone whose fingers and eyes would make them live.

On those journeys back home I became adept at reading while I walked and sometimes had a hundred pages finished by the time I turned up the Hodgsons' road. My arms would ache from holding the book out straight and I would probably have tripped two or three times and scratched my face on overhanging limbs, but I would have enough read that I could put the book down and help Mrs. H. get supper without being desperate to know what happened next.

Five months after our conversation about leaving school we had our second talk. I had not forgotten about the choices lined out for me, but I was no closer to deciding which was best than I had been the first time.

Her expression was graver this time. She started off with the biggest news first.

"Mr. H. and I are giving up the farm. His heart just won't take it, all the work there is, and my lumbago doesn't like winter better than it ever has. My brother lives in Ohio and that's where we'll be moving. George Steen is giving us something for the land, enough for rail fare anyway. That leaves you Beth to think about."

"I'll be fine," I said quickly, though the words were even more hollow than they sounded.

"Alan Steen you must surely know. Wasn't he just ahead of you in school? I saw him yesterday when I went to town and he's usually so bashful and quiet, but he surprised me since we had a nice long talk."

Mrs. Hodsgon said he asked about me but I gave this no credence. I never saw him speak to a girl in school let alone me. He played baseball but stood at the bottom of the class and never opened a book without wincing. He was gentle with the smaller pupils, he never let anyone bully them, and other than that I knew very little about him.

He is six feet tall, with boyish features, and his friends tease him cruelly about his ears. He slumps too much, being so tall, but when he finally looks at you his eyes are friendly and sympathetic. And his hair is oatmeal colored, with lots of brown sugar mixed in. He is strong, he has always been strong if you talk just about muscles. Once at school the shed caved in from the snow and he went outside and lifted the beam on his shoulders until the men could come brace it back up.

He started visiting the farm now, pretending it was to talk to Mr. Hodsgon. I remember being astonished that he could talk so easily. Most of it was about his parents who he worshipped. He was temporarily angry with his father because he wanted to go join the Canadians and fight against the Kaiser and his father said no, but I never heard him say anything else against him.

Mr. Hodgson did not think very highly of George Steen. He was said to be the richest man in town, but what did that mean up here? "He's got his head an inch further out of the mud than the rest of us," Mr. H. said. "An inch—and he thinks it's a mile."

When commencement night came Mrs. Hodsgon made a dress for me from muslin she found in her trunk. She tried her best, she looked startled and puzzled when she first saw it on me, but I loved it since I never had white to wear or anything so soft. I worked hard on my speech, I delivered it in a clear, strong voice, but it dissatisfied me terribly. It was about our futures and how bright they were, but when I looked down at the six graduates waiting to receive their diplomas, saw how dull and hopeless they looked, I knew it was all platitudes and I had chosen the wrong thing to say.

They were all going on to high school but not me. The Hodgsons were leaving for Ohio in July. My dress I would never wear again. I hate self-pity more than I do anything, but it was hard and I turned rudely away from people who congratulated me on my speech and tried not to cry. But that was only half how I felt. There was a tent set up and paper lanterns and banjo music and I saw the older boys staring at me in a way they never had before and for the first time ever I felt pretty and feeling this made me dizzy and I wanted to feel it even more.

That was one of those June evenings when the locust trees blossom even beyond what they manage normally, and the creamy tassels looked like decorations hung from the branches especially for us. They were the same color as my dress—I remember that, too. Behind the school was a grove of hemlock and we all knew that if you ducked your head and pushed through the branches you came to a secret path that led down to a soft little wildflower meadow where no one could see you. After a while people stopped congratulating me and I was alone. I could hear fiddle music starting and I was still feeling dizzy, only this time it was from the perfume of the locust blossoms which was overwhelming

Without really thinking about it, I began walking toward the hemlock grove, and without ever hearing him, I noticed Alan Steen walking right behind me. We came to the secret passage and stopped side by side. We still did not talk, though I could feel his eyes on my shoulders and the back of my hair. I knew that if I ducked through the branches and pulled the briars apart and walked down to the meadow he would follow after me, shy as he was. It did not seem just a meadow, it seemed like my future, and I was tired of always waiting for the future, always being frightened of it. That is why when Alan, getting up his courage before I did, stepped through the trees, held the branches back, reached his hand out, I took it, held it hard. I was fifteen and a half years old.

His parents decided that the wedding should be in August. The Hodgsons had left by then and so Alan's maiden aunt walked me down the aisle, tsk-tsking with her tongue the entire way. It was only afterwards that I got to know Mr. Steen. Mr. H. always described him as a cross between President Taft and President Wilson—"lard topped with preacher." And it is true, he is corpulent now, though in his younger days he had been a famous brawler and his face, solemn as it is, still bears scars. His skin is the color of old potato peels, his ears and nose are stuffed with briary red hair and his eyes always look frightened and confused without his meaning them to.

He has a business that thrives, buying up land and abandoned farm houses, ripping them apart and having Alan cart the planks down to the city where they fetch a good price. When Mr. Steen was young he had gone for wild times to Quebec and he had the fixed belief that Sherbrooke was going to be the next Montreal. If you took a ruler and drew a line on a map from Sherbrooke to Boston it went right through town, thereby assuring him his eventual fortune.

In the meantime he never worked very hard, but spent all his free time hating. He hates immigrants and Jews and negroes and professors and socialists and sissies and scientists and Democrats. None of these people demonstrate true Americanism in his opinion, Americanism being his favorite word. He could be nice enough, talking to me, almost too nice I thought at times, but when the hate comes over him his eyes harden, his neck stiffens, and his fat puffs up until he seems doubled. Where does this come from? I often wondered. His life had not been a bad one. It was like he plucked it out of the air, that was the frightening thing. Like hate had wafted in a cloud from another part of the country and, since it suited him, he reached up and pulled the cloud down.

He has his cronies, the toughest of the loggers and teamsters who are in his employ. "My troopers," he calls them. There are no Jews here to trouble or negroes, so during the war they devoted most of their energy to harassing Frenchies. Young farm boys were crossing the line from Quebec to hide from conscription, they wanted no part of England's fight, and Mr. Steen and his posse patrolled the back roads at night to capture them and send them back, almost always after beating them senseless.

Mrs. Steen is rail thin, with black hair so beautifully silky it seems stolen and a chin that looks hacked out of bone-white flint. Her lips hardly move when she talks, the words seem to emerge half-formed from the bottom of her neck. She is a miser, her fingers enjoy the feel of money which she always turns in her fingers before pocketing. She bullies the minister in church, he goes around in constant fear of what she might demand, and she will not allow a book in her house except the Bible.

She calls me "My little lamb" and all but purrs, but then she remembers that I had finished ninth grade and she had only gone through fourth and so she scowls and calls me "The professor" or "Little Miss Fancy Airs." She hates me because I will not go to church on Sundays. I told her it was Alan's one day off, our only time to walk in the woods together or go for a picnic, but this only made her angrier.

Alan listens to everything his parents say, takes it very seriously and will not hear a word against them. They bully him mercilessly, are always comparing his lack of accomplishments to his father's success. How he gave in on the house is a good example.

We planned to purchase one of the old farmhouses and fix it up. We talked and talked about how we would do this, but his parents said no, that we must live closer to town, that only rough people still lived in the hills. I remember after the wedding when we finished the miserly round of sugarcake that was all Mrs. Steen would allow. "I have a surprise for you, Beth," Alan said, turning away so as not to meet my eyes. "Mother and Father are building us a new house out by the creamery and it should be ready by autumn."

The spot they picked was three miles from town but Mr. Steen was convinced business would grow in that direction and then we would be in the center of things. The fields round about were owned by Judson Swearingen and they are wet and soggy most seasons, but there were three flat acres protected from the north wind by hills. The only neighbor lives with his daughter a half mile further on the road, old Asa Hogg who came back addled from the Civil War after all he had seen.

We stayed with Alan's parents while the house was being built. Mr. Steen would drive us out in his carriage to watch how things progressed. He was good with horses, he could calm the unruliest with a whisper, and except for the fact that he needed them for business he had no use for automobiles at all. He would bark instructions out to the workmen from the road, gesturing with the mallets of his fists. Mrs. Steen sat beside him with her head bowed praying. Praying for the house to be finished quickly? Praying for the rafters to collapse? It was going to be nicer than the house she had as a bride so she was jealous. Since her lips barely moved and her voice emerged from her neck, people in church thought she was speaking in tongues. It made me shiver and if no one was watching I covered up my ears.

The house was finished in October. Alan did not tell me until we moved in, but some of the timbers had been salvaged from the Hodgsons' farm when Mr. Steen tore it down. This made me sad but then I felt comforted and reassured, that those good people were still somehow with me. Alan painted the house red and put up a small barn and I was responsible for making everything pretty inside. I had my collection of books and Alan crafted a shelf for them which we put under the window here in the parlor. There were not very many. Mrs. H. had given me her Dickens and teachers in school felt sorry for me and sent textbooks and I had some poetry from the library they were otherwise going to discard. Not many books—and so I cherished every volume like old friends.

The workmen left a mess inside and it was many weeks before I had things straightened and cleaned. The kitchen was too big but Alan found a wide silver stove that made it cozier. I ordered a beautiful paper from the Sears and Roebuck book but I procrastinated pasting it up since I loved the bare walls just as they were. The plaster was cream colored and so smooth you could not resist running your hands along them. They gave you the feeling that they could be anything you wanted them to be, that they were just waiting for your command. Mr. Steen hired his roughnecks to build the house but for plastering the walls he sent for a gentle Italian man, Mr. Cipporino, who lived three towns south and was a master of his craft.

"Ah Beth!" he would sigh as I sat watching him work. I knew that it was not me he was sighing for, but someone he had left years ago in Italy. "Ah, mia Beth!"—and then, turning back to the wall, he would smooth his artist's hands across the plaster to make it perfect.

Mrs. Steen hated the walls, she always complained how bare and ugly they looked without paper and when was I going to decently cover them? Never, if it was up to me. Not until I understood what their smoothness was asking of me, what they wanted me to make them.

I would have liked the house more if I was not bothered by a feeling that grew stronger toward winter. What had I done to deserve something so nice? I knew about housework, I could clean and scrub all day long, and yet my labor had not earned the house and for that matter neither had Alan's. I had no one I could talk to about this. Alan could be strong at night in our room, so strong and loving in the light from our candle, and yet this would fade once dawn came and he would be timid and uncertain, letting his parents boss him or even his friends. I loved winter more than summer because in winter the nights were longer and the longer the nights lasted the longer he was mine.

A baby was supposed to come that spring, we both knew what was expected, and when it did not I had no one to ask questions of and I was left alone to suffer everyone's whispers and stares. It was then that my idea formed, though really I had clung to it all along. I know it was Decoration Day before I got up the nerve to ask.

We sat on the porch waiting to go into town. When I was little there would be a parade with all the G.A.R. veterans but now only poor Asa Hogg was left. Alan was going to drive him to town and hold him steady while he laid a wreath on the monument. I knew we would not have time alone later so I decided to ask now.

"I will put the garden in tomorrow," I said, not knowing how else to start. "I think blueberries will do well here, so we need to find out about cuttings."

Alan, who sat with his chair propped back against the railing the way he liked, grunted out a yes. A merganser splashing in the stream across the road held his attention.

"We have the house nearly done now," I said. "We shall have a family, but it may not be for some time yet."

The merganser paddled off and it was only then that he looked at me.

"What was that, Beth?"

If I was going to ask, it had to be all in one rush.

"I wrote the principal at the high school and he said I could matriculate in September, though I may have to work harder than the others to catch up. I'm ahead in reading and not that far behind in numbers. I might be able to graduate in a year and a half if I work hard. Then I could be of help to you in business and when we have children I can teach them at home even before they go to school."

Alan shook his head as I knew he would. "Please?" I said, and hated myself immediately since it was so nearly like begging.

"In September?"

"The garden will be done then, you'll be going on your trips to the city so I'll often be alone. It isn't hard to get there. I can ride Bonnie to the train station and take the local."

This time he really thought about it, I could tell by the serious way he squinted into the sun. He did not want to hurt me and yet it was difficult for him to say yes and so he ended up saying what I knew he would all along.

"I'll ask Mother and Father what they think of your notion and if they say yes then you can."

We collected Asa Hogg in the buggy and drove him to town. During the ceremony I could see Alan whispering to his parents but it was impossible to tell anything from their expressions. They drove off immediately afterwards but we stayed on for the picnic and ball game. We got home in the dark and I went in ahead with the lantern while Alan unhitched the horse.

I knew right away something was different, the violated sensation was waiting for me the second I crossed the threshold and by instinct I ran straight into the parlor to my books. They were gone, every last one of them. The Dickens, the textbooks, the poetry. There was no sign of them, the bookcase was gone, too, and in its place, for an insult, was a huge brass spittoon.

Alan came in now and I turned on him all my fury.

"Your parents did this. Your father. No, your mother."

"Beth—"

"I am going to high school in September. You can agree with this or not but I am going and no power on earth can stop me."

"Of course you can go. Of course, Beth. Why, it's a swell idea. You can give it thirty days to see if you like it or whether it's too hard." He nodded, proud of himself for coming up with a compromise. "Thirty days seems perfectly reasonable."

"I will graduate head of the class," I said, not bragging, but like a statement of fact I had to make, not to him, not even to his parents, but to myself.

I took the spittoon and carried it out to the porch, determined to throw it in the stream. There on the lawn, deliberately trampled, was one of the poetry books the librarian had given me. I picked it up, wiped the mud from the covers, held it close to my breast and took from it, not the comfort I usually found, not the escape, not the friendship, but courage.

Vera stooped to read the last paragraph, and for the last line, tucked well down into the dusty corner, she had to kneel. The words were spaced closer together the nearer the floor they dropped. The girl, Beth, had obviously been very determined to fit in as much as she could. The script that had started off so neat and prim changed toward the bottom. The ink was blacker, as if she had pressed harder on the pen; the dots on the *i*'s and the crosses on the *t*'s had drifted right from the beginning, but now they often blew over into the next sentence.

Vera got back up and touched the wall again, as she had many times while reading. The words seemed warm, or at least she fooled her fingers into sensing warmth. If she closed her eyes, concentrated, she could feel the shallow, all but imperceptible, gouges left by the nib of Beth's pen.

She would have liked to uncover more, starting on the wall to the right, but she was too tired now, not only her wrists but her understanding. Taking the putty knife she peeled back a strip near the top, just to assure herself there were indeed more words. Who had written them was plain enough now, the girl had gone to great lengths to explain. What it was meant to be wasn't as clear, but it appeared to be an explanation or confession. Why she had done it was harder to guess, though with patience, with more wall cleared, perhaps that would become obvious as well. Some of her motives were understandable enough. The feeling of having something cooped up inside demanding its way out. The comfort of confiding in the future. Wanting to put words down just to find out if they made any sense. Anyone could understand this, really anyone, you didn't need matching pain of your own.

That night, for the first time since arriving, Vera slept without waking up for her midnight vigil. She took a walk around the house in the morning, trying to see it all from Beth's point of view, how it must have looked in 1920. The lilac near the kitchen seemed ancient, it was so high and tangled, and she remembered reading that in the old days wives would plant them near a window just to enjoy their perfume. Some of the shade trees must have been a hundred years old, too, they were so high and rotten. When she walked around to the front she could look up the road to the small gray farmhouse—Asa Hogg's place, the addled one, the man who had seen too much of war. She walked across the grass, trying to imagine discovering a favorite book trampled in the mud—then, guessing, decided that right there must be the spot, halfway between the porch and the road near a lichen-covered flagstone sunk well down into the grass.

Too much had been added or subtracted over the years to make the yard look original. All the debris, the rusty swing set, the corroded lawn chairs, seemed to be from the Fifties or Sixties, and it overwhelmed anything earlier. Looking back at the hills or even up at the sky gave Vera a better, purer sense of it—what it must have been like to be young and spirited in a land that was emptying out.

When she went back inside, before starting on the next wall, she searched through the last lines from the night before. Reading, she had been taken out of herself, her absorption had come as a relief, and yet the old danger still persisted, of tripping back to the present on a random phrase. She found it now, Alan's compromise—*"Thirty days seems perfectly reasonable."* It was as if she had put the words there herself, they fit so ironically. Thirty days, the length of Cassie's sentence. Thirty days for smiling. Thirty days in an army stockade for smiling at the wrong time, the wrong place. Thirty days for Cassie to prove herself in prison. Thirty perfectly reasonable days for Vera and her walls.

As before, the only way to escape this was to busy herself working. The parlor was perfectly square, which meant this next wall was the same breadth as the first, which meant a day's worth of scraping. It was both easier and harder, knowing what was hidden underneath. Impatience made her hurry, always fighting down the temptation to just hack the wallpaper away, regardless of what it did to the plaster, but at the same time the writing made things easier, since the words seemed actively helping her, demanding their way out, pressuring up on the strips of paper while she pulled. By late afternoon she had the entire wall uncovered, and there was still enough sunlight filtering through the window that she could read without needing the lantern.

The distance to school never bothered me. Our town does not have enough pupils for a high school of its own and neither does the next town so it meant going three towns south to where the first big railroad bridge crosses the river and all roads meet. Alan had a truck now for business and he would drive me to the station where I would wait for the morning milk train. There were no cars for passengers but the trainmen were friendly and would let students ride in the caboose. It was thirty minutes ride and then I would walk the rest of the way uphill another twenty-five minutes. This was fine, since I still remembered how to read as I walked and it was while trudging up and down those steep sidewalks that I did much of my work.

On the first day, not knowing any better, I wore my best frock. This made the other girls decide I was rich and stuck-up, though I felt like a bumpkin compared to them. But when I climbed up the marble staircase, found the locker assigned to me and went to my first class I was almost bursting from happiness and nervousness combined, since it was by far the bravest thing I had ever done.

My first class turned out to be disappointing. I found a desk near the front and the boy behind me, when the door opened and the teacher came in, poked me in the shoulder. "Miss Crabapple," he whispered and for the rest of the class I thought that was her name. She had a sour frown, sour eyes, sour wrinkles and she made us sit with our hands folded so it was like I was seven again and back at the county home.

That was history. Mathematics was better and then came lunch which I ate alone under a tree and then it was time for English composition. The classroom was on the fourth floor off in a corner so it seemed exiled from the rest of the school, a secret room or garret that made me feel like Aurora Leigh living in London writing her poems. I felt a pleasant sense of anticipation even before the door opened and the teacher walked in.

He was a young man, not that much older than the seniors, but he gave off an immediate air of authority and command—it was only later we found out he had been an officer in the Great War. He was handsome in the way men are who can force away their homeliness by sheer will power. You did not notice his big nose or over-large head or bad complexion—his blue eyes and spirited way of staring blinded you to the rest. You sensed that his face was not the barrier or shield that most people's are and you were looking directly in to who he was, who he really was, with no excuses. Likeable is the handiest way to describe this. Likeable but with an edge.

His hair was sandy and surprisingly unkempt. His eyelashes were the longest, most doe-like I had ever seen on a man and he seemed self-conscious about this, because he was always touching them, almost primping. He dressed shabbily, in a brown suit that hung loose from his shoulders. Combined with his dusty army shoes and half-tied tie it made him look absent-minded, which was the very last thing Peter Sass ever was.

He sat at his desk with his head in his hands moodily staring out at us, then, as if electricity had just switched on inside his chest, sprang to his feet and started marching up and down the nearest aisle.

"Who's your favorite author?" he demanded, stopping at the first desk.

"Uh, Longfellow," the boy stammered.

"Who's your favorite author?" he demanded, stopping at the second desk.

"Eugene Field," the girl said primly.

"And you?"

"Edgar Rice Burroughs."

"You?"

"Maria Susanna Cummins."

"You?"

"Samuel Clemens."

The teacher stared down at him.

"Sawyer or Finn?"

"Tom Sawyer."

That took care of the first aisle. He marched down my aisle next, where there were only four of us.

"Who's your favorite author?" he demanded, stopping at the first desk.

A blonde boy sat there, new like me and very handsome—the girls had been pointing at him, nudging each other and giggling before the teacher came in.

"Oscar Wilde," he said in a voice of complete and utter boredom.

Mr. Sass, obviously surprised, hesitated, then moved on to me.

"Browning," I said before he could even ask.

"Mr. or Mrs.?"

"Mrs. of course." I wanted to stand up for myself right away.

"Who's your favorite?" he said to the student behind me.

"Jack London."

"And you?"

"Theodore Dreiser."

Mr. Sass returned to the chalk board, folded his hands behind his back, drew himself up straight like he was about to issue orders to his platoon.

"This is a large class and we have permission from the principal to divide it into sections. One group will immediately transfer to Miss Gleason's class while the ones I call out will remain here."

He walked down the aisle again, brandishing a ruler.

"Stay," he said to the boy who liked Wilde.

"You too," he said to the boy who liked London.

"And you," he said to the girl who liked Dreiser.

My heart sank because he walked right past me toward the other aisle, but then he abruptly swiveled, came back to my desk.

"And you."

This is what it became, just the four of us in that dark, drafty classroom hidden away under the eaves. How Peter arranged this no one knew. We heard that he worked very hard with his other classes, took a personal interest in every pupil, and I saw for myself how furious he would get when Lawrence, the blonde boy, made fun of them and called them dolts. Even with us he was strict, he would call roll and demand we answer, and then we had to stand up and salute the flag. After that he would relax, treat us as equals, and I think he saw our special class, coming at the end of a long day, as his reward for drilling the rules of grammar into future shop owners, druggists and clerks.

We started with four but were soon down to two. The girl who read Dreiser, Ellen knew lots of names I had never heard before, not just American authors but ones in Europe. Though I was frightened of her for being so smart and she was frightened of me for already being married, we tried hard to be friends. Her parents had sent her there from a village even more remote than ours, but the room and board turned out to be so dear that she had to leave school and start work.

The boy who liked Jack London was quick and very funny but his banker father wanted him to take business courses, not waste his time on novels and poetry, so he soon left as well. That left just two of us—and yet every day, the moment he stepped into the classroom, Peter would take out his attendance book and call roll.

Lawrence was the other pupil, Lawrence Ridley Krutch. Like Ellen, his parents sent him into town to board since he lived so far away. He never talked about them or his home, seemed already done with that part of his life, and kept his eyes firmly on his future. His brilliant future. He made sure everyone knew it was going to be brilliant. For he was by far the smartest pupil in school and saw no reason to pretend otherwise. Unlike every other boy, sports held no interest for him and he was outspokenly contemptuous about the "clodhoppers" who played football and baseball.

His hands were soft and delicate, not rough like the other boys', and his eyes were a flirt's, so lively and dancing. The girls adored him but he had no favorites, seemed happiest when five or six surrounded him in the hall and giggled at his jokes. He was very nice to me, I was the one girl he let be his confidante, I suppose because he thought of me as an experienced older woman. When I had trouble with mathematics he made sure he sat with me after class to go over every problem until I understood. When he learned I was an orphan he asked me all kinds of questions about what it had been like and no one had ever done that before.

"Why didn't you take down their names?" he asked. "The names of all the people who mistreated you."

"Their names? I've tried hard to forget them. Why would I want their names?"

"For revenge," he said—and then he shook his head in amazement, that I could be so innocent and naïve as to forgive them.

I worried about him sometimes, the contempt he was too free in expressing, his carelessness toward life. He knew his future was bright, that his brains would carry him far from these hills, but for the time being he seemed in no hurry. Except for his weakness for sarcasm, he seemed perfectly content to be the smartest, handsomest boy for a hundred miles around.

Peter, once Lawrence and I raised our arms and yelled "Present!", lectured while pacing back and forth in front of the chalk board, rubbing his hand across his forehead like he was polishing off his thoughts before releasing them. He wrote on the board so vigorously the chalk was always snapping in his hand and it was my job to collect the pieces after class and line them up again in the tray.

As I said, he talked to us as equals, though this was more for Lawrence's sake than mine. I had to struggle to understand, I was so far behind. But I enjoyed having to struggle. All my life I had been surrounded by people who wanted to make life as small as they possibly could and now for the first time I was with a man trying to make life as large as it could be made. Often in the middle of his talk he would go to the window and point outside, showing us that this is where the world of ideas was, not here in this stuffy classroom. The more excited he grew about his subject, the softer his voice became—Lawrence and I were always leaning forward to hear.

What he enjoyed talking about most was American litera-ture. This was not some dead mummified thing in a textbook, he told us, it had not been buried with Washington Irving or Feni-more Cooper, but was going on right now out that window—why, it was coming into maturity as we spoke, entering the golden age everyone had been awaiting for so long. Edward Arlington Rob-inson, Edith Wharton, Sherwood Anderson, Robert Frost who was writing about these hills, even Booth Tarkington who should not be ignored. We should pay very careful attention to every word they wrote.

He told us the best thing about American authors was their faith in progress and their believing that America was the best chance mankind ever had for achieving that progress, not just in material things but in basic human values like honor, respect, tol-erance and mercy. American writers believed that men, even sim-ple men, could be trusted to set things right in time. That had al-ways been the American wager, he said, and if writers were sometimes disillusioned, it was only because reality had not yet caught up with the dream.

He got excited, rubbed his forehead, rumpled his hair, moved to the window and pointed outside.

"Right now, understand? Out there, out across the country, men and women not much older than you are creating the books that teachers will tell their students about in a hundred years time."

Listening to his passion, it was impossible not to believe that these authors and poets were writing right outside on the high school's lawn. I had never heard anyone talk like this and while I always felt ignorant and naïve and very much behind, I felt this less so as the weeks went on. "He who believes in the potential of life must also believe in its realization and be predisposed to work for it," Peter told us. I wrote that down on my tablet and all the way to the train station stared down at it and by the time I got there understood.

He went out of his way to recommend books to us. He told me about Celia Thaxter who wrote beautifully about living on an island off the coast and then recommended Mary Austin who wrote about her early life in the Western desert land and her later years working at a settlement house in the New York slums. The Land of Little Rain the first one was called and No. 26 Jane Street was the name of the second. The library did not have either, but when I came to school that Monday there they were gift wrapped on my desk and Peter, trying hard not to grin, pretended he had no idea where they came from.

Peter never said very much about himself, not in those first weeks. He had moved often since leaving the army. This was his fourth teaching position in two years and each move brought him further north toward the edge of things. He rented a house out by the river. He liked trout fishing and he had a gramophone collection with lots of Rosa Ponselle. Along with his books this was enough to keep him happy. He told us more than once that lonely as things were here he wanted to make it his home.

The trains ran more irregularly in the afternoon and I often got home after dark. Alan would meet me at the station and carry my books. He held them in a strange way, at arm's length like they might hurt. He seemed confused by them, puzzled that I could find so much meaning in things he had always been frightened of.

"Your thirty days are up today," he said once we reached home. "I'm glad you had the chance to try. Maybe some time in the future you can go back."

I knew I had to keep my temper. They did not seem his words and I knew where they were coming from.

"Tomorrow I go back. It's only Thursday."

"Well, I'll need to ask Mother and Father about that."

"A wonderful idea. Let's invite them for Sunday dinner."

It was important to call their bluff but I regretted it once they came. Mrs. Steen went on an inspection tour of the house, frowning at all the fixing up still needing to be done. The fact the walls were not yet wallpapered especially bothered her—in her view of things a woman who lived in a house with bare walls was equivalent to a woman who paraded around naked. She touched the plaster as if smearing it with something dirty from her fingertips and later I went around scrubbing every single spot she touched.

We had a little comedy when dinner started. Alan went to a side chair, leaving the position of honor at the head of the table for his father, but I got there before he could, held the chair back and said loud as I could, "Alan? Why don't you sit up here?"

So. There was a mood. Mr. Steen speared some roast off the platter, then started in on his favorite topic—the fine work they were doing down in Washington, rounding up foreign agents, throwing radicals in jail, putting a good healthy scare into people. Attorney General Palmer deserved a medal for standing up for real Americanism. Why, he could do good work right up here if someone alerted him to the situation. There were teachers in the high school who were stirring things up, trying to change things, importing foreign thoughts. He heard there was a new teacher who acted as their ringleader, a Mr. Ass or Mr. Rump or something unmentionable like that.

Alan, who had sat silently eating his turnips, now looked up.

"Mr. Sass. Beth has him for English."

I nodded. "He's the best teacher there."

Mr. Steen stared over at me—the scars seemed to coil upwards from his cheeks to his eyes, narrowing them into purple slits.

"He's a Democrat," he said, spitting out the word.

"No," I said calmly. "He hates Wilson and worships Teddy Roosevelt."

"He's a radical."

"No. He was an officer in the Rainbow Division and fought in France."

"He's a New Yorker."

"He was born in Bemidji, Minnesota where it's even colder than here."

"A Jew."

"The son of a Presbyterian minister."

"I bet he thinks we're descended from apes."

I was going to say something terrible but before I could someone interrupted.

"He's a bachelor!"

Mrs. Steen said this, or, in her manner, croaked the words out her neck. She made it sound like the worst accusation yet. By this point I just wanted to laugh at them and I had to busy myself with the rest of dinner or perhaps I would have. When I came back from the kitchen Mr. Steen had switched his venom to an easier target. A librarian two towns over was stirring things up, handing out radical literature, giving young people dangerous ideas. When I asked him what sort of radical literature he frowned mysteriously, as if that was for him to know and me to guess. I asked again and this time he mentioned Uncle Tom's Cabin.

"I think it's time me and my boys went over and paid her a visit," he said darkly. "Just a little visit by real Americans to show her what's up, give her a good healthy scare."

Mrs. Steen must have worried he had gone too far—she wiggled her eyes back and forth as a warning and he changed the subject with a coarse laugh.

"I nearly wet my pants laughing today, the sight I saw."

Alan knew his cue. "What sight was that, Father?"

"Francine Toliver climbing over a fence. Why she must weigh three hundred pounds just counting her bottom."

It was the worst dinner I ever sat through and when his parents left Alan and I had our first real quarrel.

"Someone saw you walking out with him," he said. This was laying in bed with the lights out long after I thought he had fallen asleep.

"With who?"

"Your Mr. Sass."

"It's a long way to the train station, Alan. He helps me carry my books just as you do once I get home."

"Like Mother says, he's a bachelor. People will get the wrong impression. I don't want you seeing him outside class."

"Is that your idea or your parents'?"

He took so long to answer I thought he had fallen asleep again.

"I have ideas, Beth. They may not come as quick as yours do, but they're there just the same."

Autumn had been rainy and cold but the following week it turned warm again and the sun slanting through the leaves felt like a gift the sky was laying against your face. Indian Summer people said—it will not last long. On Tuesday I was sitting on a bench outside school, alone with my lunch as usual, when someone called down to me from a fourth-floor window.

"Stay right there, we're coming down for you!"

It was Peter and Lawrence who between them had decided it was far too nice to have class indoors. We walked downhill past the match factory which was empty and derelict, then, after passing the abandoned clothespin factory and climbing a fence or two, came at last to the railroad tracks that ran along the river.

It was breezy, the wind streaked the water, but if anything it felt even warmer than back at school. Lawrence tried catching the maple leaves as they fell but had a hard time, they swerved so at the last second. Peter tried and did much better. In a short time he had a bouquet which he handed me with a courtly flourish. He took my hand, then, acting a bit bashful, as if this were too bold of him, reached for Lawrence's hand, too, so we walked three abreast on the bed of cinders that flanked the tracks.

We stopped where the trees opened into a meadow set high above the river's surface. You could tell from the way the bank was worn that it was a favorite spot for picnickers and fishermen. Someone daring had shimmied up a tree and hung a hempen rope for a swing. It was a tall silver maple leaning from the bank, so the rope dangled a good way out. You could easily picture children playing on it in summer, reaching with a forked branch to tug the rope back to the bank, grabbing hold of it and laughing as they launched themselves over the water to land with a mighty splash. The end of the rope swing, the part that dangled over the river, was tied into two thick knots. Lawrence, pointing, said something strange.

"It looks like a noose, like a hangman's noose."

It cast a pall and he seemed to know it because right away, jumping up on a stump for a stage, he started in with his impressions of all the teachers. Peter tried not to laugh but in the end it was too much for him, especially his Miss Crabapple, and he applauded even louder than I did.

When Lawrence finished, Peter tried persuading him to go down the river bank with him to search for pike sunning in the shallows, but Lawrence was timid when it came to things like that so Peter went by himself. It was a steep, perilous climb down and Lawrence and I were certain he was going to tumble in, but at last he made it and lay there on the last narrow shelf with his arm extended out over the water as far as it would go. He was as still as a heron, concentrating, and then suddenly his hand dipped and came back out holding a silver minnow! He lifted it above his head as if it were a real trophy, then lobbed it as far out into the river as he could.

He is showing off again, I decided, and who else could that be for but me? It made me feel girlish, seeing that. With the sun shining down on him, outdoors, he gave off even more authority and strength than he did in his classroom and I wondered at myself that I had ever thought of him as homely.

After he climbed back up we lay quiet on the grass. Above us the maple leaves were layered atop each other like fans the breeze kept peeling back, so more sky became visible even in the few minutes we stared. I wondered if I should tell Peter about what the Steens had said at dinner, but they were so ridiculous, their accusations so wild and unfounded, it seemed that saying them out loud would only be making the danger more real than it actually was. In the end what did their accusations amount to? That ignorant bigots knew his name.

As beautiful as it was there, Peter had not forgotten this was supposed to be a class. From his battered army bag he took out a slim, rose-colored volume.

"A friend sent me this while I was in France. I carried it with me the whole time I was there. It became my talisman—my rabbit's foot. There was one shell. Well, I won't tell you what it did to us. But the first thing I did when I shook the mud off was check my pocket to see if it was still there."

He opened the book, then hesitated. What he was going to share with us seemed so important that he could not bring himself to begin.

"Picture a girl, not much older than you Beth, standing on a hill above the coast looking out toward sea."

I nodded, closed my eyes, not because I had to in order to imagine, but because I thought this would encourage him to start.

"Renascence," he said quietly. "By Miss Edna St. Vincent Millay."

At first I was more conscious of his voice than I was the poem, he read so wonderfully, but then the words disappeared and all I was aware of was being inside the experience itself. The girl in the poem looks out at the wide view of ocean, sensing the islands and the horizon, and it is very simple that way until, in a stanza of magic, the sky presses down on her and forces her into the ground, so it is as if she is dead. She has to suffer all the pain of the world. "I saw and heard and knew at last," she says, "the how and why of all things past." When the pain finally eases, when she begins to sleep serenely for evermore, a torrent of rain bursts from the same sky that crushed her and washes her back to life. She embraces all the sights, smells and sounds of the world she had once taken for granted, all the beauty after all the pain, ruing the day she ever thought of life as trivial and small.

Peter, reaching the last verse, closed the book and read by heart.

"The world stands out on either side,
No wider than the heart is wide
Above the world is stretched the sky
No higher than the soul is high
The heart can push the sea and land
Farther away on either hand
The soul can split the sky in two
And let the face of God shine through
But East and West will pinch the heart
That can not keep them pushed apart
And she whose soul is flat—the sky
Will cave in on her by and by."

I would need Miss Millay's gift for words to describe what her words did to me. Never had I heard anything that made me feel that the author has seen so deeply into my heart. I knew what smallness did to the soul, how difficult it was to fight this off. I knew that hunger for beauty and how alone it could make you feel. I trembled, literally trembled, to find she knew this about me and so much more.

Again! I felt like shouting but Peter had already moved on to read more poems. Ashes of Life one was called and When the Year Grows Old and then, as his gentle little finale, Afternoon on a Hill which made it seem like she was sitting there with us.

"I will be the gladdest thing
Under the sun!
I will touch a hundred flowers
And not pick one
And when the lights begin to show
Up from the town
I will mark which must be mine
And then start down."

Laying beside me on the grass, Lawrence seemed as moved as I was. "Tell us about her," he said.

Peter shrugged. "I don't know much. She published her first poems when she was a student at Vassar College. She can't be much more than twenty-five now. My friend in New York knows her slightly. Her new book of poems is coming out before Christmas."

When he read poetry Peter trusted us to understand and he seldom offered us any interpretations. He seemed too moved to bother trying to teach us, or perhaps, prompted by the poem, he decided that he needed to teach us something harder and the only way to do this was by changing the subject.

Without any preliminary he started talking about his experience in France, something he had never done before. His regiment had been stationed west of a town called Romagne where the fighting was brutal. Night attacks mostly. Noise, blinding lights, poison gas. The wounded calling for their mothers. Hardly knowing which side was which.

"I did well there," he said honestly, without the slightest trace of bragging. "The boys respected me, not because of any of my virtues, but because they needed someone to look up to and there were no other candidates in sight. I found I could take the shelling better than most, which I put down to my complete lack of imagination. We had men in the division from all over the country—that's why they called us Rainbow. Many were poor farm boys from the high plains or the Appalachians who had run away just for the adventure. They were sorry they had now, the trenches were so horrible. But they carried on without complaining and that's why I came to love them."

He told us stories about several, giving us their names and hometowns and what brave, selfless deeds he had seen them perform and how far too often he had to crawl out of the trench to recover their bodies. They were in the famous fight for Chatillon Hill and half his platoon had perished climbing the slope. It was afterwards, lying exhausted with the survivors in a shell hole fifty yards from the German trench, that he saw something that haunted him still.

"I don't expect you to believe when I tell you this. At first it was nothing more definite than that cloud you see blowing in right above us, but then gradually it became more substantial, touching the earth, gaining strength seemingly from the corpses, coiling upwards and darkening. There was gas in the shell holes and fog and smoldering flares and all kinds of strange and terrible vapors, so it wasn't unusual for the men to see visions. But what we saw that night was more real than anything we witnessed before."

The streamers of fog and gas furled themselves around an axle that was black and hard, so at first it was like watching a huge pole being erected in No Man's Land from which swirled long skirts of shredded fabric the same dun color as the dead men's tunics. The top third of the pole swelled, became fleshy—it seemed a huge mushroom or a grotesquely misshapen face.

Next to him, the sentry raised his rifle ready to fire but Peter stopped him. What was there to shoot? The other soldiers, sensing that something was up, crawled to the lip of the hole and stared. These men, who could face down any German attack, now wore expressions of absolute horror. For the pole seemed to divide itself vertically into two and then two again and then another two, so there were soon more than a dozen, only they were no longer poles but the gigantic outlines of men. Not ordinary men. Devils.

"I know what you're thinking. That it was all an illusion, that we had been fighting in those trenches too long. And perhaps it was an illusion, but the illusion was a real one, which is not the contradiction it sounds. For the first time in my life I realized Evil, pure Evil, really exists in the world. Not a man there didn't believe that this is what we were staring at—that the devil was emerging from hell and dividing himself up into a band of identi-

cal brothers. He was surprisingly like what you see in bad illustra-
tions, he even had a long black cape, but it was his face that convinced you he was the real thing—never again do I want to see
such a face. He, or rather they, seemed to be a bit confused by the
lay of things, even devils couldn't figure out No Man's Land satis-
factorily. But they soon got their bearings and started off."

"Off?" Lawrence said. He had listened to this as silently as I
had and I could tell he was just as moved.

Peter nodded. "The twelve devils moved off in different directions, high stepping over the barbed wire. One turned and headed
in the direction of Germany. One turned south toward Italy. One
went toward Belgium and another toward England. One seemed
perfectly content to stay there in France. One headed northeast
toward Russia."

Lawrence forced himself to smile. "Well, at least none headed
toward the good old U.S.A."

Peter closed his eyes. "Two did."

We were silent—for a long time we stayed silent. Peter's story
was so powerful it seemed to influence the weather or maybe it
was the changing weather that darkened his mood. The puffy
clouds hardened now, became mercury color trimmed with white.
The wind swept around from the north and strengthened, so the
canopy of leaves blew down onto our laps. The river changed, now
that the sunlight had left it. It flowed faster, more purposely, as if
it were carrying not just its water south, but everything about the
valley that was beautiful and fragile and not tied down.

Peter, seeing me shiver, leaned over and covered me with his
jacket. We lingered for a few minutes yet, reluctant to let go the
afternoon. They must have read the river like I did, that it was

escaping, flowing toward the future, because the future is what they began talking about.

Lawrence told us he had been admitted to Columbia University in New York to begin a special accelerated program in the spring. He did not bother being modest about this since, he explained, it was a perfect opportunity for a boy with his abilities and ambitions. He would not miss small town life at all—he was very funny about this, very sarcastic and mocking. As usual with Lawrence, the more he went on the handsomer he became. It was as if only sarcasm could fill his face with energy, make his beauty come to life.

"Boobus Americanus!" he yelled toward town. "Sunday school yokels, Odd Fellows, the glorious commonwealth of morons! Goodbye to you all! Goodbye Philistines! Goodbye Boosters! Goodbye Klu Klux Krazies who reek of dung!" He waved his arm around. "Goodbye mills, goodbye cows, goodbye town!"

Peter and I both laughed, though we wanted to shush him, he yelled so loud. Peter, when it was his turn, spoke more quietly. He was not sure yet, he had only been here a few months, but he was beginning to think this was as good a place as any to make a life. There were no book stores within a hundred miles, true, but other than that it had many of the qualities he had been looking for. He wanted to teach and be with his books and take walks in the hills and these seemed perfectly attainable goals. He was afraid Lawrence was over-valuing the rest of the world. Here where people needed each other they had to be more tolerant of differences, not less.

He said it again, as if wanting to stamp it on the day and make it permanent.

"I want to enjoy my books and teach and every once in a great while be blessed with students like you."

It was my turn after that, my turn to speak of my future, and while I could sense them watching me, waiting, I had nothing.

"I need to go now," I said. We all sprang up together and beat the leaves from each other's shoulders. It was the happiest afternoon I had ever spent. I wanted to tell them that but felt too shy.

We walked back up the railroad tracks and they waited with me for the train. The Indian Summer that had lasted so long was over now. The clouds lowered, the wind gusted, icy pellets blew down—and thus began the harshest, cruelest winter in a hundred years.

Once again, as on the first wall, the spacing between lines tightened as the writing dropped toward the floor. Once again, as with the first wall, Vera was kneeling by the time she finished. It took more effort than reading a book, with the constant adjustments needed to make out the words—stepping close where the script was faded, stepping back again when her eyes began blurring things up. Her back hurt from stooping, her neck was sore from following the lines toward the top, and now her knees ached, too, so her whole body was involved. The ironic thing was that her fingers and wrists had toughened considerably; a week's worth of scraping had burned all the soreness out, so she felt she could go on stripping wallpaper forever if that's what it took.

At times, reading, she felt a tugging sensation, not just on her eyes, not just on her heart, but on every part of her still capable of responding to the world. Take me out of myself! In the middle of the wall she had made this appeal and almost immediately it had been answered. A different era. A different consciousness. Different wounds. The sensation of inhabiting these was addictive, her imagination wanted more and wanted it instantly, and it was only the fact she hadn't eaten anything since breakfast that made her decide to take a break.

There was housekeeping to attend to. Strips of paper covered every inch of the parlor floor and she had to sweep this and take it outside to her little fire. The dishes, the few she had used, hadn't been washed in two days. The lantern had to be refilled, but she knew how to do this from camping, and this time she brought the kerosene in with her so she could work deep into the night.

She slid the ladder over to the next wall, took an appraising squint at things, decided to use the broadest scraper first. No words emerged from under the first piece she peeled, but this only made her smile. Beth and her indentations! But when she pried the next piece off there was nothing under that either, and nothing beneath the next one, nothing but bare plaster all the way across. Puzzled, she climbed down one step, chipped at the paper just enough to lift it back. Nothing. Nothing on that wall. Nothing, when she investigated, on the fourth wall either.

She felt so disappointed that her shoulders literally sagged, but there was only one possible explanation. Beth must have begun her wallpapering on these two walls the very first day she started. She must have thought long and hard about writing on the plaster, the idea had tempted her and frightened her simultaneously, and her inner debate wasn't resolved until she had the first half of the room, the first two walls, entirely papered. Then, not able to contain herself any longer, she began writing on the bare third wall and then the bare fourth—Vera's first wall and

second. Continuing on around the room would have meant
stripping off the wallpaper she had already hung, and instead of
doing that Beth would have taken her story to a room where the
walls were still bare and inviting, which meant, logically, the
next room down the hall. It was the only sequence that made
sense.

The next room down the hall. Vera had peeked in on her inspection trip, but this was the first time she had ever entered the
room itself. It surprised her, it was so feminine and cozy, and she
decided immediately that it must have been, not a den, but a sewing room, a place of refuge. The knotty pine paper darkened it
terribly, but the floors were the lightest, most delicate looking in
the house, with maple boards that had been milled and chevroned
to form interlocking triangles, then polished to a jewelry box
sheen a hundred years of traffic hadn't managed to erase. It even
smelled vaguely of wax, and brought back memories of her grand-
mother and Easters and brand-new shoes.

Things grew shabbier higher up. A fan-shaped window had
lost most of its glass, and the dampness streaming in found the
lantern light and turned it plasma yellow. The molding, delicate as
it was, hung down in strips, as if someone had gotten mad at it
and yanked. And then of course the wallpaper, which seemed an
even worse desecration here than in the front parlor.

Which wall to start on was difficult to determine, but, using a
book as her template, it made sense to try to the left of the door
and work her way around to the right. She went back to the parlor
for the ladder and tools, balanced her way up three steps, wiped
the sweat from her forehead, shook the hair from her eyes, and
started scraping.

Almost immediately she came upon a word, which surprised her, since it was Beth's habit to indent. Still, she didn't think much of it—if anything, she was pleased to have located the writing so quickly—but that changed with the second word, revealed when her scraper got lucky and pried off a six-inch strip all at once. It wasn't Beth's handwriting, it was nowhere near as neat, and the ink was different—ballpoint, and blue instead of black.

I can't

The surprise came doubled—surprise at finding it, surprise that her first reaction was irritation. When she had first discovered Beth's writing the effect had been of a woman stepping into the room and pronouncing the old-fashioned word out loud, *credence*, and now, having become used to that voice, comfortable with that voice, she was suddenly called upon to listen to another one that already seemed louder, more shrill. But almost immediately her curiosity took over. She dug away near the ceiling and found another word and then another, followed their prompts right across the top of the wall until she had the line entirely uncovered.

I can't tell a story like she can.

The ink was thin and cheap-looking, recalling those plastic Bics she used when she was in middle school. With the pen held that high to write, there were places where the ink had dried up altogether, the letters becoming little more than cursive white scratches. Some letters were script and some were printed, but it was impossible to figure out what guided the logic, and the line itself slanted sideways like a ramp. It was slapdash, even drunken—the handwriting of someone who cared nothing for rules or consistency.

Who had written it was more obvious than it had been with Beth. It could only be the woman who had lived in the house back in the Sixties, the one who stripped off the three layers of old wallpaper, then covered up everything with the knotty pine and wedding cake that had been on the walls ever since. In walking through the house, in exploring the overgrown garden or following the dead-end path out to the wall, Vera had sensed this woman's presence much more strongly than she had any of the other owners, though this had never crystallized into a definite image, much less a name or personality.

Someone had lived here fifty years ago who had labored mightily to turn it into a replica of the suburban homes she saw in the women's magazines and on television, with a swing set, lawn chairs and barbecue, the rusty remnants of which now littered the weeds. She had tried the same trick inside with the wallpaper, working hard to make things modern, scraping off the layers she must have considered horribly old-fashioned and dull. And then, like Vera, she had discovered Beth's words. Discovered them, read them—and then covered them up again, but not before writing on the walls herself.

I can't tell a story like she can. More diffident than Beth, but was that just a pose? You could read the sentence as a brag, not so much the words but the forceful, don't-give-a-damn way they were scrawled. *I can't tell a story like she can*—and then the unwritten add-on that seemed implicitly attached: *but I'm damn well going to try.*

Vera was too tired for any emotion to stay with her for long—surprise circled back to irritation, that this woman should dare interrupt her connection with Beth. At the minimum, it meant more work. She crossed over to the next wall and peeled off just enough paper to find the same sloppy handwriting, then checked the next wall, then the one after that. It was the Sixties woman's room all around. Beth, unless she had given up completely, must have skipped the sewing room for the next room down.

This was the back parlor, identical to the first, only smaller and shabbier, with a tent of cobwebs held up by a plastic milk crate, empty beer cans, a whitish-green powder dribbled to the floor by wasps. Jeannie had said something about squatters and maybe this had been their space. A plywood shelf jutted out from the wall with a stack of paper plates that looked petrified and a faded copy of a 1967 *TV Guide*. Someone had made a halfhearted attempt to brush everything into a corner, then given up—the broom still lay in the middle of the floor where they had dropped it, the bristles chewed off by mice.

But it made perfect sense that, back when the room was new, Beth would have preferred it to the sewing room. The walls were larger, giving her more space, and the light was better thanks to the window. Immediately, under the very first strip she peeled, Vera came upon her writing again, up high on the top left-hand corner of the left-hand wall. For all her impatience, there wasn't much she could do about this until morning, not unless she wanted her arms to drop off. On her way upstairs, she stopped by the sewing room, stared in toward the dark. It was silly of her, childish, but too many spirits were popping out at her now, and she shut the door as tight as it would go.

Stripping went fast in the morning. She placed the radio in the middle of the floor, found her Quebec station, pulled the ladder over, started in. Enough mist had oozed through the window that the wallpaper felt damp, but this seemed to help, since she managed to peel off some of her longest strips yet. What helped even more was establishing a three-part rhythm she could maintain right across the wall. Edge of scraper to get cut started, little nicks and nudges to loosen things, blade pressed back as far as it would go. What—happens—next? the rhythm went. By the end of the third wall she was actually reciting this out loud, like a work song that made things easier, not only by helping her concentrate, but holding off the darker moods that were always waiting to rush into a vacuum.

By lunch she had the first two walls uncovered and by dinner all four. Now that the words were there for the reading, she hesitated, wanting to read them immediately and yet feeling unaccountably shy. She went outside, used the hose for a shower, went upstairs for her robe, came back again for the lantern. Such ceremony!—and yet she felt unable to read the walls without it. I'll need to dress in white if this goes on much longer, she decided. But it was only because she felt so strongly the need to give something back to this girl, not just through her scraping, but by the purity of her attention.

It was nearly Christmas when I had my idea. Peter told me Miss Millay's new volume of poetry was coming out and I decided it would be the perfect gift for him. He had opened a wider world for me, the world of books and poets and ideas, and now I could go out into that world and bring part of it back for him. He complained about there not being a book store within a hundred miles, which left me grasping—a hundred miles WHERE? I could not ask him without giving away the surprise so I ended up asking the only other person who might know.

Miss Norian, the school librarian, was the meanest woman in school after Miss Crabapple. She attended the same church as Alan's mother and gave the minister an even harder time. She did not enjoy loaning out what few books the library had. Two days was all you were allowed and if you returned it late you were not permitted to take out another one all term.

So, I had to get up my nerve to approach her. She seemed to like me or maybe it was because she knew I was related to Mrs. Steen and wanted to curry favor.

"I have a question about the library," I said. "If you want to order a new book, where do you order it from?"

This surprised her—it was many years since she ordered a new book. The wen on her nose quivered in suspicion.

"I sent to Brattleboro. To the Elm Street Book Store." She squinted at me through her spectacles. "Number 41 Elm."

"Would a book arrive in time for Christmas? If I telephoned and had it sent?"

"Christmas? Why that's only three days, Beth. I would say there is no chance of that at all ... How is dear Mrs. Steen? She does such fine, such charitable work. Please give her my sincerest regards, will you promise?"

I never considered not going. Having the idea I had to pursue it to the end. Alan was working with his father dismantling a farm house north of town. He had his new truck, no one else in town had one so big, and he was always calling me outside to see how much lumber he managed to pile on its bed. On Friday he would be away all day, which meant I could take the milk train into town just like I was going to school. When I got there I could wait for the express which ran straight down the river to Brattleboro. It was good service. If I walked directly to the book store from the station and did not dawdle I could easily be back in time to fix Alan his dinner.

I had just enough money saved from what Alan gave me for groceries. He always left in the morning before I woke up, but this time I rose with him.

"What time will you be home?" I asked when I helped him on with his shirt. The truck was running outside and he stood by the window proudly watching its steam.

"We might cut the day short, it's up to Father. See those clouds? We're due for a storm. You'll stay close to the house where it's warm? It's good that school is on vacation." He took a meaningful glance at the bare, unpapered walls. "Maybe you can have a go at things?"

"Do you remember me telling you about Ellen Lavoie, the girl who left school to work? She wrote and we're meeting for lunch today as a Christmas treat. I may be back a little late."

The steam coming from his truck went from clear to sooty and Alan seemed concerned over that. Pointing toward the sky with a be-careful gesture, he disappeared out the door.

I had never lied like that before, not even over small things. I felt guilty, but it was more complicated than that, and I sensed I had taken my first step out into the world even before my journey started. I did take Alan's advice over one thing. He had a long woolen coat he wore when it was below zero and though it came down almost to my ankles I knew it would keep me warm no matter what the day brought.

The trainman, Zack Perkins, was surprised to see me since there was no school. He shouted out a warning, "No heat in the caboose, Beth!" but with Alan's coat I managed fine. When we came to town, instead of walking to the high school as usual, I purchased my ticket, crossed the platform and waited for the southbound train. I could see it for a long time before it arrived, with its black plume of steam, and when it pulled into the station I jumped back to avoid its sparks.

There were few passengers. Four commercial travelers sat playing pinochle on a sample case, on their way home to Boston after a trip to Montreal, and they smiled pleasantly when I walked past. Further down was a family with a wicker hamper settling in for a long trip. I balanced my way to the next car and sat on the left so I could watch the river. For a long time I was convinced the train must be headed north, not south, the land seemed so empty and forgotten. A half hour after we left I was further from home than I had ever been before and yet it looked scarcely different. Solitary farm houses set high against the hillsides. Forests that had been cut down to stumps. Now and then a little village, nestled inside a bend in the river or perched above a falls. All the way to Brattleboro I saw only one single person, an ice fisherman in a red parka hunched motionless over his hole.

And yet this could have been France, I was so fascinated. I sat with my face touching the window and kept twisting around since I wanted to see everything, not miss a single detail. The valley spread apart when we got close to Brattleboro, the train slowed down, and between one moment and the next there were people everywhere. Hobos warming their hands over a fire. A gang of workers repairing the tracks. Boys out with their slingshots, aiming good-naturedly at the coal car. Autos waiting at crossings for us to pass—more autos than I had ever seen before and trucks that made Alan's look tiny.

When the train stopped I climbed down onto the platform and asked a newspaper boy which way Elm Street was. It had begun snowing and the streets were slippery, but the town was crowded with shoppers getting ready for Christmas. Walking up Main Street I saw my first negro man ever and just beyond him my first Chinese man and then my first flapper, her hair bobbed and shiny, her dress stopping just above her knees, a cigarette jaunty in her heavily rouged lips. A policeman dressed like an admiral directed traffic and seeing me put his hand up imperiously and made everyone stop so I could cross. I felt self-conscious, Alan's coat was so long and heavy, but then I realized that no one could really see me, that there were so many people on the street I passed unnoticed. I liked that feeling. It made me think I had been dropped invisibly into a magic city that I could enjoy all I wanted without having to explain.

Elm Street was three blocks off Main, lined with small shops. All the display windows were decorated for Christmas, with wooden trains or hand-carved creches and tinsel-covered trees— the falling snow touched their glass with a delicate, fleecy pat. I stared in at all of them but they were nothing compared to the window of the last shop. I had to rub the frost with my glass to see inside. There was nothing displayed there but books and yet they were more colorful and happier looking than anything in the other windows, with their different sizes and shapes, the way they slanted against each other, supported each other, propped each other up. Some covers were coral and others were butter-colored or a very deep rose, and they blended into one long extravagant mural that ran right along the glass. By walking down it I could make out an ocean liner and doughboys and Lillian Gish and a man leading a camel and girls with parasols and an old woman walking hunched through a picket fence and a man with his hands on his hips staring defiantly from a cliff and President Harding and the Four Horsemen of the Apocalypse riding four skeleton steeds. The authors' names made a flowing scroll of their own and I smiled when I found one I recognized. I had never seen so many books in one place at one time and when I considered that this was only the display window, that there were likely to be hundreds more inside, I felt dizzy from happiness and shyness combined.

The bell tinkled when I opened the door. I stamped my shoes on the mat, shook back my hair to make sure no flakes would fall on the books. A round turtle of a man was down on his knees searching a shelf near the cash register and a pleasant looking woman stood on a sliding ladder writing on a ledger but there was no one there to stop me from looking my fill.

It resembled a city, that was what struck me hardest. Not a book store but a city. The shelves were arranged in parallel rows and pressed close together like city streets, so there was hardly room to slide between. That made it crowded but in a good way, as if the city were bursting from energy and excitement. The aisles were the streets and the shelves were the buildings and the books were the inhabitants, and, as in the window, they came in all shapes and sizes, textures and colors. Too crowded and sloppy someone else might have complained but I realized the moment I entered the shop that this was its magic, that there was simply no way to display books without making them beautiful. Throw them in the air, let them fall, the effect would have been beautiful. Stack them end on end it would be beautiful. Pile them backwards. Books can not help being what they are.

It was hard, I wanted to pick up every single one and read them right there or collect an armful to bring home. I could not do this, I barely had enough money for the book I wanted, and so, not to be tempted, I went over to the woman and asked for help.

"I would like Edna St. Vincent Millay's new volume of poetry," I said—and being able to say this out loud made the whole trip worthwhile.

The woman wore her glasses on a chain and now she tugged them up her nose to see me sharper. I think my coat surprised her. That someone wearing a shaggy farmer's coat could have heard of a famous poet.

She smiled kindly enough. "Do you mean A Few Figs from Thistles?"

I nodded.

"We don't have any in yet. It's proven very popular in New York. I did place an order."

She must have seen my disappointment. "Wait a moment," she said, climbing backwards down the ladder. "A new shipment came in this morning I haven't unpacked. Novels mostly, but perhaps, just perhaps. Let me check in back."

She was gone a long time. When she returned she carried something cupped in her hands like a baby kitten.

"One copy! It's your lucky day, miss."

I handed over my money and she handed it back all wrapped. "Just a moment," she said, glancing out the window. "Let me add an extra layer for the storm."

I wanted to touch it, open the pages, and I was sorry she had wrapped it so quickly. I had never bought a book before and decided that this must be the proper etiquette, not to look at a book until you brought it home. I thanked her for her help. The turtle-like man stood behind me with an armful of novels and I felt jealous and happy for him, too.

It should have been faster going back to the station, since I now knew my way, but the snow blew sideways and it was impossible to walk without wincing. The train pulled late into the station—the locomotive's silhouette was nearly doubled by the snow clinging to its hood. When the conductor put down his box for me to board I heard him call out to another conductor further along the platform. "Let's hope they have the St. Bernards ready, Mike!"

There were more passengers this time, mill girls returning for Christmas to the farms where they grew up. They were dressed in the latest fashions, trying to act sophisticated and aloof, but giggling, too, they were so excited at going home. With their gifts and bundles it was hard to find room and I had to wedge myself in near the middle of the car.

We were well out of the station before I got up the nerve to free the book from its wrapping. The jacket was simple. A Few Figs from Thistles by Edna St. Vincent Millay, with red bands boxing the title and softer red highlighting her name. The covers, when I slipped back the jacket, were blue—sea blue, I decided, though I have never seen the ocean. They had a rich texture, since especially fine cloth had been used. I ran my fingers along the front, then down the spine. The book felt good in my hands, not too heavy, not too light. I opened it to the middle, enjoying the perfect way the paper felt, stiff but not too stiff, pliable but not too pliable, with a faint grainy quality that made me sense the trees and forests from which it came.

I took my time with this and only looked at the back of the jacket when I felt ready. Miss Millay's photograph was very small. She was even younger than I imagined, not much older than me and much prettier. Her hair was bobbed but a rebellious curl was fallen loose over her ear. Her eyebrows were thin, she had no defenses over her eyes, so they looked very vulnerable. Her small hand was up against the side of her small chin and below it was a glimpse of lacy black collar. She had a perfect Mary Pickford mouth and her nose was delicate and very feminine. My friend, I decided, though I knew it was silly. My new best friend.

I intended to keep the pages uncut but I knew Peter would understand my temptation. For a cutter I used my comb. I cut all the pages, holding the book open on my lap, then when I finished went back and read the book straight through, trying on the weight and feel of the words the same way I had the covers and paper.

After that I read through it again, this time more slowly. To the Not Impossible Him. The Philosopher. The Singing Woman from the Wood's Edge. MacDougal Street. I loved all the poems, especially the way she seemed to be talking very simply right to me and then suddenly deepened the meaning so I had to grasp. But it was there when I grasped. She tutored me as I read, never went so fast and far my understanding could not catch up.

I loved the sonnets best. I knew they were sonnets because they were fourteen lines and Peter had taught Lawrence and me how to recognize their rhythm. I decided to memorize one so when I gave him the book I could recite it out loud. It was nearly impossible to pick a favorite, at least not until I came to the last one which was perfect.

"Oh, my beloved have you thought of this:
How in the years to come unscrupulous Time,
More cruel than Death, will tear you from my kiss,
And make you old, and leave me in my prime?
How you and I, who scale together yet
A little while the sweet, immortal height
No pilgrim may remember or forget,
As sure as the world turns, some granite night
Shall like awake and know the gracious flame
Gone our forever on the mutual stone;
And call to mind that on the day you came
I was a child, and you a hero grown—
And the night pass, and the strange morning break
Upon our anguish for each other's sake."

Even with the girls talking away on either side of me I soon had it by heart. "I was a child and you a hero grown." I recited that to myself over and over again a hundred times.

Absorbed in the book, I was slow to realize something was wrong. The silence alerted me first—the mill girls had stopped their chattering. They sat straighter than before and looked out the window in absolute terror. These were farm girls and you could add to that whatever hard conditions they knew from the mills and yet they were terrified by the storm's ferocity. The train had slowed down but if anything it rattled even more than it had when it was speeding and I realized it was from the wind—that the wind was blowing furiously, bringing with it the hardest, thickest, most malevolent snow I had ever seen.

We had left Brattleboro at one, which meant it must be four now and yet the dark was already total. The lights in the train went out and soon the heat failed, too. All the girls, dressed in their city best, began shivering. The conductor marched down the aisle with a grim expression, brushing off their questions. "Delay!" he shouted from the end of the car. "Dee . . . eee . . . lay!"

We finally started up again, the girls resumed chatting, but then it became like a giant was rapping his knuckles against the window while his dog grabbed us between its teeth, worrying us this way then that. After ten minutes we stopped again, this time for good.

There were sobs and screams from the flightier girls. They did not like that it was dark. The older ones seemed resigned, they were already unrolling their bundles searching for thicker clothes. I was warm in Alan's coat but wanted to scream louder than any of them, just because I was so frustrated and worried. Not from the storm but the delay, what it would mean if I was marooned.

"How long will this be?" I asked the conductor on his next trip down the aisle.

"The drifts have us blocked."

"I have to get home."

"We're here for the night, Miss. It will be cold but at least you'll be safe. We have coffee brewing in the caboose and we'll bring that around for you. I suggest that everyone make themselves comfortable."

He said this kindly and his voice stayed calm. But I could not take that for an answer because if I did then everything, all the plans I had constructed so carefully, would come crashing down. Portents of doom were what the heroines of those novels I read as a girl were always experiencing—and now here it was my turn, the portents were real and powerful and bewildering, since I could not understand what the doom would consist of, only that it would come if I stayed on that train.

If we were three hours north of Brattleboro then it meant we had to be close to town where the high school was. The tracks were up high, exposed to the worst of the storm, but things would almost certainly be easier down on the main road. I wrapped the book up again, pressed it down into the coat's deepest pocket, then walked quickly to the rear of the car so I would not have time to lose my nerve. The door was frozen, it took shoving to pry it open, but then I got my knee and shoulder against the edge and really pushed.

I tried letting myself down slowly but the steps were icy and I tumbled off. It did not hurt, the drift was so deep, but snow got down my collar and turned to ice water against my skin. I felt in my pocket for the book and felt reassured that it was safe. I had come down near the front of the train. The locomotive, so arrogant and unstoppable, had butted its snout into a drift three times as high, so it now looked very meek. Steam whistled from the stack but it sounded soft and plaintive, as if the engine were sobbing in mortification.

I slid down the embankment, spreading out my arms to keep from going too fast. There was a band of alders bent into hoops from the snow but I ducked through them and gained the road.

The drifts were not as high as on the tracks, though the snow was still over my knees. There was a crossing gate festooned with icicles, but no sign of traffic—any autos would have been quickly swallowed. With the wind blowing from the south it meant I must keep my back to it in order to head north. I pulled the coat collar up high as it would go, but that left most of my hair exposed and the icy pellets soon made it feel like tangled lead.

Where the road rose the traction was treacherous and where it dipped the wind collected even thicker drifts. Every fourth or fifth step I had to stop and catch my breath, though that was hard with the cold squeezing my lungs. The wind made so much noise it was almost silent. It was like the locomotive had started up again, two locomotives, ten locomotives, they were speeding down icy rails right over my head, yet all I could sense of them was their rushing, belittling power, not their noise.

It was hard staying calm. The more exhausted I became the more my fancy started working on me and it was this loss of control that frightened me most. At one point I thought I saw a bonfire, imagined voices cackling in glee, decided it must be hobos, drunken hobos, so I turned away from the road and tried a detour through a swamp. That was a mistake and it took me a long time to grope my way back. In the willows ahead of me appeared a very still shape—a doe sinking to her knees, the weight on her forehead simply too much to bear.

I had read that to keep your courage up you should always whistle, but when I tried it my lips were far too cracked and dry. What worked better was remembering winters when I was little and how I used to walk back to the Hodgsons' farm from the library reading a book the entire way. Miss Millay was in my pocket, I was not going to take her out, but I recited to myself the sonnet I memorized on the train. "Some granite night" was the phrase I kept saying, since I was up to my waist in one now, with snow as hard and sharp as shredded stone. It seemed to warm me, the literal truth of it, and then I remembered one of her couplets that helped even more. "Let us go forth together to the spring; Love must be this, if it be anything." In my stupor, my exhaustion, it became my destination, the only thought my head would allow. I am going forth with my lover to the spring I told myself, over and over until it made no sense. Going forth. Forth. Forth to the spring.

I found another trick that helped. Instead of just carrying Miss Millay's book, I convinced myself that I was carrying her in my arms, my newest friend, and she was light and lithe and yielding—not a burden but something that lightened my way.

I do not know how long it was before I saw my first light. I was reluctant to believe in it, since I was convinced I was hallucinating. Very tiny, no bigger than a match—a yellow flame, one that grew steadier, less lambent, the closer I got. The town! There were suddenly more lights, so it was like a Christmas tree had blown over and scattered its candles either side of the road. I knew I was safe now or could be if I went to one of the doors and knocked, but all the courage I found in myself was reluctant to just quit. Off in the distance, dark and blocky, I could make out the high school and past that came the first shops, but they were deserted in the storm and in some respects the last half mile I walked was the hardest and loneliest yet.

I had never been to his home before but I knew where it was. On the edge of town near the river, the last in a row of three. A cottage more than a house—it was snug and secret looking behind icy vines. A candle shone from an upstairs window, though there were no lights below. The knocker on the door was frozen so I used my hand. It was not long before Peter came to the door, wearing a silky green robe. He was surprised, but he got over that instantly, seemed ready to start teasing me about something, and then that expression changed, too, once he put the light on and looked at me, really looked at me. Shock, concern, tenderness. They blinked down his face in three successive flashes and I realized for the first time what walking through that storm had cost me.

"I've brought you this," I said. I had practiced saying it all day.

I reached down into the coat pocket and brought out the book. I unwrapped it for him, though my hands shook from cold and something more than cold. He took it, stood staring down at it, and his smile, when he looked back up again, was everything I had dreamed it would be.

"Beth," he said, taking my hands, drawing me inside. "Dear Beth."

He held the book up to the lamp, nodded, then very carefully placed it on the mantle over the fireplace and squared it away just so. All his concern was on me now. Outside, I had been able to force the cold away, but once I came into his parlor I began shivering uncontrollably and thought I would fall. He drew me over to the fire, turned me so I was facing it, my back toward him, then gently began removing my clothes. He started with the coat, which was stiff as armor, lifted off my blouse, his hands expert and tender, then kneeled so he could remove my skirt. He stood up again and from behind began kneading my bare shoulders trans-

ferring his warmth deep into my skin. After a few minutes I could
sense his lips very close to my ear. "Can you remove everything
else?" he asked. "I'll be back when you're ready. No, here—take
this first."

He stepped away, then came back with a thick woolen sweater. I nodded. I heard his footsteps going up the stairs and so I did
what he told me to, took off the rest of my clothes and put his
sweater on, which was thick and scratchy and fell down below my
hips. The stairs squeaked again. I looked shyly up and there coming down the stairs beside Peter was Lawrence, wearing the same
kind of silky green robe, rubbing the sleep out of his eyes and not
looking happy at all.

"Why hello there, Beth."

It did not seem like the Lawrence I knew, or rather it seemed
like him but in an exaggerated form. His expression managed to
be arrogant and coy and jealous and friendly all at once. He and
Peter had brought blankets which they wrapped around me, then
led me gently but firmly over to the couch. Peter left for a moment, then came back with a mug of tea. The two of them sat
beside me in their matching robes, none of us saying anything but
staring toward the fire, the only sound in the room being the
crackle of its flames. I was confused, it combined with the cold to
make me dizzy, and then when the blankets and tea did their
work there was just the confusion. I remember seeing Lawrence's
school books on the table and thinking that they had not just
been casually dropped but stood between bookends like they had
been there a very long while.

"You need to sleep now," Peter said. Never had I seen his eyes
look kinder. He shooed Lawrence off the couch so there was room

for me, then put his arms under my legs and lifted me around. I was exhausted, I must have fallen asleep before they disappeared upstairs, but I kept my eyes open just long enough to see Peter come back to the mantle and take the poems.

When I woke up it was still dark though the clock read seven. Christmas Eve. I rubbed at the frosty window and saw golden Venus. My clothes were draped over a chair by the fire and were warm when I put them on. Before leaving I walked around the room making sure to tiptoe. There were not as many books as I thought there would be, but almost every one was folded open and turned upside down as if they were all being read simultaneously. Other than that, there was not very much. Mementos of his time in France. A few French coins. A cheap plaster replica of a saint. Ivory cufflinks. A phrase book issued to officers. Medals, scattered across the bookcase with the lesser souvenirs.

I was lucky because the rollers had already been over the road and I was able to walk on the crust. The morning milk train had not yet left and the trainman waved me back toward the caboose. There was less snow on the tracks the further north we went and by the time we got to town there was hardly any snow at all. This frightened me, though I could not say why. That despite the blizzard it had not snowed here even a little.

When I climbed down from the caboose I saw Alan's truck. He got out, walked around the front, held the door open. "I've been waiting here all night," he said when I got in. "I knew you would come back and I didn't want to miss you."

He tried saying this tenderly, but it came out as an accusation. He looked colder, more exhausted than I did, but when I tried giving him his coat he wouldn't take it.

"I knew you would come back, Beth."

Three times he said this which could only mean he had been saying it to himself all night. We drove to the house without saying much more besides that. Mr. Steen's automobile was parked out in front. Alan did not seem surprised to see it there. "Go in," he said, again trying to sound gentle, but nervousness had him now and it came out rough.

Mr. and Mrs. Steen stood waiting in the back parlor, here against this wall where I can still sense their shapes. Mr. Steen had a new coat for Christmas made of fur and it seemed to shrink him, make him smaller, like an animal withdrawing into his pelt. Mrs. Steen had a new coat, too, and it was as thin and cheap as his was expensive and plush. And yet it seemed to enlarge her. She acted excited and not in a good way—never had I seen her eyes shine so bright. But enlarged is not the proper word. She looked bigger than that, more satisfied, as if she had swallowed hate for breakfast. She looked engorged.

Alan had walked me into the room but now he separated himself and stood with his parents against the wall so it seemed like I was facing a jury.

"Where were you last night?" Mr. Steen demanded, with no preliminary.

I was not afraid to stare them down.

"In town," I answered. "I was trapped there by the snow."

"What snow?" Alan and his father asked simultaneously. Mrs. Steen, for her part, stared toward the window and the brilliant blue sky.

"The blizzard. I couldn't walk any further. Peter Sass took me in."

Mr. Steen scratched his belly under his coat. "Why would he do that?"

I knew if I told them about the book they would not understand and if they did understand then they would hate me. I said nothing.

Mr. Steen's bullying instincts took over now, making his chest and shoulders swell back up to their normal size.

"The Jew? The radical? The agitator?"

I stared him straight in the eye. "He took me in. I brought him a book as a gift."

I could not help saying that, though I regretted it immediately—the hate in their eyes went deeper than anything I had seen so far.

"Tell the truth, Beth," Alan said. He bowed his head, preparing himself for the worst.

Mr. Steen cut him off. "Oh, a book is it? A married woman visits a bachelor's bedroom in the middle of the night to read him a book? A pretty name for it. A book!"

"Nothing happened."

"You lie!"

I should have fought back harder, gone over and spat defiance right straight into his face, but I was still exhausted from fighting the snow. Weakness made me desperate and more than anything I needed someone's help.

"Lawrence was there. He can tell you about it. Ask him."

Alan looked puzzled. "That boy in your class? Lawrence?" He turned to his father. "There's a boy in her class named Lawrence." He tried remembering what I had said about him. "Very handsome. Very smart."

Mr. Steen was slow to take this new fact in. I could see his brain working—he even rubbed his hand on his forehead to help it along.

He spoke very slowly and more to his wife than to me. "A school boy. At the teacher's house. At midnight. A pretty schoolboy."

He then did something I had never seen him do before—he put his arm around Mrs. Steen's shoulders and drew her close. They talked too soft and fast for me to make out what they said. Alan was part of the conference, too, though he only ducked his chin toward them without speaking. After a long time their heads split apart again and Mr. Steen began buttoning up his coat.

"Stay here," he said. "Mother Steen will keep you company."

He took Alan's arm and guided him out through the hall. A few seconds later we could hear Alan's truck cough to life. Mrs. Steen was furious she had been left behind. She stared with enough intensity to pin me to the wall. "Don't move!" her eyes commanded, and then I heard her spitting into the telephone out in the hall. When she returned she was almost beside herself from excitement. She paced back and forth across the floor muttering to herself the way she must have when speaking in tongues. The words oozed from her neck like they always did, only this time they seemed covered in gristle and blood.

"Just a good scare is it? Just a good scare? You'll miss the fun you will. Stay here they say, watch the girl they say, no place for a woman. No place for a woman? No place? No other place. No other place! Just a good scare? We'll have a party with just a good scare. Women aren't invited, women can't watch? Women can't watch? We'll watch our fill, the good Lord will watch with us."

The angrier she grew the faster the words came out, to the point I could no longer understand. After a few minutes a horn sounded out on the road. She grabbed my wrist, not bothering to be gentle and pulled me after her outside. A black truck was waiting, shabbier than Alan's, driven by a man I recognized as one of the roughest of Mr. Steen's loggers, feared for the way he used his belly as a weapon during brawls. Mrs. Steen hurried over and issued her instructions, jabbing his stomach in emphasis. He nodded, got behind the wheel, and then Mrs. Steen grabbed me by the hair and forced me onto the back seat next to her.

Mr. Steen's man drove east toward the village, which puzzled me, and I only became frightened when we reached the main road and swerved south. Mrs. Steen kept urging him to go faster. The road was clear but then we came to where the snow had fallen and he had to stop and put on chains. Mrs. Steen, if she noticed the snow, said nothing. While she waited for the man to finish she drummed her knuckles on the back of the seat and stared toward the steering wheel as if debating whether to take over. She cuffed him on the back of his neck because he drove too slow and cursed him when he skidded. For an hour we drove that way. We passed the high school. We came to the railroad tracks and the river and then suddenly I knew where we were heading.

Trucks had trampled down the snow and parked atop their own dirty tracks. A child's shredded kite, forgotten in the summer, stuck out of the drifts like a yellow marker showing which way to walk. Mrs. Steen walked on one side of me and the driver on the other so there was no chance of my bolting. There was a band of birch trees, then an abrupt ridge, and it was not until we crested this that we could see the river. It was the color the deepest cold can take on without actually freezing—gray beyond gray, so it was impossible to look at without shuddering. There were icebergs, too, long swelling humps, and they bobbed up and down in the current like racing ponies.

Twenty yards back from the bank, in the flat spot where the three of us had our picnic in October, stood a group of ten or eleven men. My first reaction was laughable. I thought it was a ball game—that these men had decided on the coldest day of winter to play baseball. Then, when they dragged me closer, I saw they all wore parkas and gumboots, so I knew they were loggers, Mr. Steen's men. They are driving something downriver I decided, logs or pulp, but the cold slowed my understanding and it was another few seconds before I saw things clear.

In the center of their ring, prone but with his arm up as if fending off blows, lay a naked man. Lawrence! He was wet and it made his whiteness even more startling, though the veins in his arm were as red as licorice. I could not understand why he should be wet and naked and cringing in the snow, my eyes could not accept what they were seeing. One of the men kicked his ribs and laughed and then another man took off his parka and threw it at him, not in charity but disdain. Lawrence fumbled desperately to pull it on—already the wetness was turning to ice.

I tried running to him, but Mrs. Steen grabbed my arm and yanked me back. Lawrence's humiliation was not what I had been dragged there to witness. On the edge of the river stood another group of men, the roughest of Mr. Steen's loggers plus Mr. Steen himself. There was someone in the middle of their ring and like

Lawrence he was naked, though he was not lying down but standing tall and proud like he was at attention.

"Peter!" I yelled.

The driver shoved me sideways and Mrs. Steen clamped her hand over my mouth. Off to the left under a big pine, well apart from the two mobs, Alan stood by himself watching. I know he did not see me, not yet. Peter did not see me either, nor could he have heard my shout over the river's roar. What frightened me was what lay draped over Peter's shoulder—the dangled rope of the tree swing, the one we had seen on our picnic, the one Lawrence compared to a noose.

Responding to an abrupt gesture from Mr. Steen, two of the toughs grabbed the rope and forced it down over Peter's head and shoulders, cinching it tight across his chest. His turn now, I suddenly realized. His turn after Lawrence's, though I still did not understand for what. At Mr. Steen's barked command, the men pulled Peter to the furthest edge of the bank, then positioned themselves behind him squatting on their heels.

I turned away so as not to see but Mrs. Steen anticipated this and by twisting my arm forced me to look. "Sodomite!" she hissed, pointing. Peter saw me now, I am certain he saw me, because he raised his hand just as the two men who had hold of him shoved him hard toward the river. The tree rope tightened on his chest and his feet came off the bank, swinging him sideways out over the current, then careening him back. He did not struggle to fight this—from first to last he did not struggle. He bounced off the lip of the bank and pendulumed back again, this time even further out, and as his full weight came against the rope it snapped apart right above him and he fell into the river with less splash than a stone would make but only a quick leaden sucking.

He rolled over like a log, rolled a second time, and I could see him trying still to raise his arm through the current. Mr. Steen and his men staggered over to the bank and stood there staring in cow-like stupidity, but I think even before my scream Alan must have started running. He forced his way through the snow to the bank and ran downstream trying to keep Peter in view, tugging off his jacket then his shirt. Where the bank steepened he must have made his decision because he dove into the river head first. We could see him splashing at the ice, trying to keep it from forcing him under, but the current would not let him go further out than he already was. The men finally started running—after Alan, not Peter. They could have saved themselves the bother. Far downstream, just where it seemed he would disappear after Peter around the first bend, we could see an exhausted Alan stagger alone through the shallows back to the bank.

"He's saved!" a man yelled, one of the ring guarding Lawrence. Then, realizing his mistake, he kicked viciously at the snow. They seemed ashamed of themselves, this group, and now they were all taking off their parkas to cover Lawrence's nakedness, warm him back to life. He was crying, sobbing, retching, though he could not have known yet about Peter.

Behind me, Mrs. Steen put her lips to my ear and whispered like she was stuffing hate in just as deep as hate would go.

"You saw nothing, understand? You were home with all of us, we baked a cake for Christmas, sang songs and didn't once leave the house. Understand? Understand woman! You saw nothing, you were home with the three of us, we baked a currant cake for

Christmas, sang carols, stayed in the house the whole livelong day."

I nodded just to be rid of it, that moist hateful breath down my ear. The men pulled Lawrence to his feet and took him back to one of the trucks. Someone else ran to help Alan. Mr. Steen and his cronies walked backwards from the river, using pine boughs to sweep snow over their boot prints. Mrs. Steen and the driver tugged me over to the truck and forced me in.

I was sick after that. All the novels I read as a girl, in almost every one, the heroines come down with brain fever after suffering their tragedies. It was not brain fever I had, it was only the 'flu, but it still kept me in bed for a very long time. Alan would not leave my side at first, though we never talked. One night I woke from my delirium and it was not Alan sitting by the bed but Miss Norian, the friend of Mrs. Steen, and she was tearing out the pages from a book and using them to blow her nose. With the other hand she was stroking back Peter's hair which rested on her lap like a soft brown pillow—and I hated her for daring to touch him, though I knew it was only my fever.

Gradually I grew better and then one day Alan said he would leave me alone and go off to work. Later that afternoon I felt strong enough to walk downstairs and after resting a bit in the parlor I decided to go outside for some air. There was a path shoveled through the snow to the road. I was all the way there, turning to come back, when I noticed a black truck parked fifty yards away. There was a man behind the wheel and he did not seem to be doing anything but watching. Watching the house. Watching me. As I got better, as Alan began leaving me along for a longer time each day, the truck remained there, or a similar truck, with a similar driver, so I was always watched.

And I knew that this is how it would be. It would always be that way. It would be that way until I gave them what they wanted.

"I have wonderful news," I told Alan on Valentine's Day when he brought me candy. "We will be having a baby. There can be no mistaking the signs."

"A son! Why I'm sure of it, Beth!"

"I'm sure, too."

The next day when I went out for my walk the truck was gone.

How long I can fool them I do not know but it will not have to be for long. Alan feels confident enough to go on a trip to the city with lumber and will be gone five days. "I'll hang the wallpaper while you're away," I told him. "At last I have the time and when you come home it will be finished, every room."

"You'll be careful on the ladder?" he said, leaning over to kiss me.

"I'll be careful."

"Wonderful. Why that's just wonderful, Beth. Mother will be so pleased."

I will begin hanging the paper the moment I finish this sentence and I will work very carefully until every wall is covered and I will leave my story behind and I will never stop hating them and in springtime when they least expect it I will go.

Three

VERA stayed in touching distance as she read. Move close to the wall and the words blurred. Move back and they became squiggles. By the time she finished she was running her finger under each line like a first-grader, tracing out the story all the way to its end. Her arm ached from doing this, her back hurt from standing, and she felt chilled in a way even a July night couldn't touch.

But this was nothing compared to how the last word affected her. The last word detached itself from the wall, took on shape, form, and substance, to the point she had the sensation she wasn't reading it but accepting it in her hand. It was a better trick than any poltergeist could manage, any goblin—it was a real hand that had come out to take hers, warm, girlish, pleading. Sensing this, she grabbed hard, closed her fist around the word trying as best she could to summon all her courage and send it back ninety years.

go

She grimaced, she concentrated so hard. And almost immediately, as if a century was nothing, she felt a matching pressure
back. A message—but could she read it? None of the meanings
she came up with described the sensation adequately. Sisterhood,
but that seemed too girly-girly and easy. Kinship? That was closer.
Solidarity? An old-fashioned word she had never quite understood, but she understood now and she closed her eyes to it,
clenched her hand so tight she felt dizzy and had to reach out to
the wall again, this time to keep from falling.

It didn't last long, the hand sensation. The word released her,
flattened itself back to its place there on the bottom right corner.
A punctured *g*, a deflated *o*. She left the lantern on the ladder,
kicked through torn wallpaper toward the door, stumbled down
the darkened hall through the kitchen out to the yard. The word
had released her from its grip but not its meaning. *Go* it said. *Go!*

She started for the car, remembered the key was upstairs in
her purse. And even if she had the keys there was no way to out-
drive what she was feeling. Instead, she pushed her way through
the gate and began walking north along the road's weedy shoulder. The ground was wet, swamp plants and nettles swung heavily
at her legs, but she kept going, concentrating on each step so as
not to slip. The fireflies were finished now, there were no chartreuse motes, but the crickets had started up. Their sound wasn't
the pleasant one crickets were supposed to make, but something
so harsh and percussive she covered her ears.

She walked until the house was well behind her, turned to
get her bearings on its light, then kept on until she came to the
neighbor's house, the one she often stared at on her breaks, where
Asa Hogg had lived, the Civil War veteran. And no one since,

judging by the look of it. If Jeannie's house resembled a haunted house in a bad Hollywood film, then this one looked plucked from a fairytale, where the forest clasped everything in its enchanted embrace. The moon's brightness exaggerated the effect. Vines not only covered the siding and roof, they seemed to be the only thing keeping them from collapsing. A birch tree grew through the broken boards of the porch and lichen covered its shingles in silvery fur. Saplings stooped and twisted to get inside—one branch grew into one window and looped back out the next. The forest wasn't just hiding the house but eating it, gulp by greedy gulp.

She swung her hands at the vines until she opened a path to the nearest window, found a stick, made a swirling motion to clear away the broken teeth of glass. But when she peered in she could see nothing, and it took her several seconds to realize that this was because there was nothing inside to see. Where the floor had been was only the bitter damp smell of dirt; where the walls had been was nothing but ugly little dunes of plaster. There was no furniture, no sign of habitation. Time's nibbles had swallowed the house whole.

She was pushing her way back through the vines when a car drove past on the road. This happened nine or ten times a day, but never once at night—the traffic in 1920 must surely have been heavier. Its headlights sliced across the house but missed her legs. She had a glimpse of the driver's silhouette and he seemed to have a girl's head leaning against his shoulder like in the old days when that's what girlfriends did. The car slowed down near Jeannie's house—were they looking for a place to be alone? The light, small as it was, must have scared them off, because whoever was driving floored it now and the red taillights shrank into insignificance and disappeared.

Jeannie's house? No, Beth's house. Beth's house. Beth's.

She had never really considered it from the distance before, not at night. The kerosene lamp she had left in the parlor threw rays out the window that resembled a campfire's, fan-shaped and yellow. In the blackness, it was a brave and defiant sight, like someone was puffing on embers to keep them alive. Higher, with a crisper light, she could make out Scorpius and the swarming white band of the Milky Way. And it seemed the same even there—that a spirit was puffing and blowing to keep them alight.

There was nothing to explore in Asa Hogg's house, no stories or secret messages. She walked back to the road, then stood there hesitating. *Go.* The imperative had taken her what—half a mile? She wondered how far it had taken Beth, that word added so defiantly on the end. Had she made it to the city? Had it been everything she dreamed of or did forces conspire to drive her right back?

She might have fled there herself, had she gotten in the car. Had she gotten in the car she would have driven all night to Boston's airport and not come back. She was disappointed at the slowness of things, there was no use pretending otherwise. The job was barely half finished, there were two rooms left that had to be stripped even before she started on the papering, while that other job, the healing business, had hardly progressed at all. She wanted walls that were impassive so as to become impassive herself—but why had she ever imagined walls were impassive?

She thought of it again—the tactile sensation of grasping Beth's hand. Comfort had been exchanged, in the deepest way possible, and it hadn't just flowed from her hand back through time, it had flowed the other way, she had gained solace from listening to Beth's voice. It was far more comfort than she had been able to send or receive through Cassie's hand. In the stockade, in the miserably small room where they were allowed to visit after her court martial, they had been separated by a wire mesh screen that kept them from touching. The thirty minutes allotted them was over, Vera was nowhere near dealing yet with the shock and incomprehension that came with their talk, and yet, by instinct, needing it badly, she reached her hand out to touch Cassie's before getting up to leave.

She was letting her hair grow long again—never had it looked so shiny and beautiful.

She remembered thinking that, of all possible things, and then a second later, worrying that maybe Cassie would turn and walk away with no gesture whatsoever. Then very slowly she did move her hand—low to the mesh where Vera's hand already waited. They hadn't touched. They hadn't touched the way she touched Beth because a quarter inch of wire mesh in an army stockade is thicker, more impermeable than a hundred years' worth of time.

But she was a liar, to remember it that way. When it came to touching, the truths a mother and daughter can exchange through their hands, she had been glad that the mesh was there.

She could lie to herself. She could fool herself, too. For when she woke up next morning it was with the fixed intention of stripping the sewing room wallpaper without paying any attention whatsoever to the writing underneath. Beth's story still held her. The emotion could only lessen gradually, it didn't need to be forced away by someone new.

Her resolution lasted about as long as it took to peel off the first strip. The new woman's voice was simply too loud and insistent to ignore. *I can't tell a story like she can.* Plain enough. But how was she going to tell it then?

The handwriting was sloppy, bold and fast, like the letters were racing each other, tripping over themselves, staggering back up again, making their erratic way to the finish line there in the corner. Whoever wrote it had a fondness for cheap ballpoints and liked different colors—by the end of the first paragraph she had already used blue, black, green and red. The lines sloped down, then rose back the other way like a crude drawing of waves. When she became passionate or angry she pressed too hard, pockmarking the plaster or even gouging it; the walls in the sewing room were in much worse shape than in the parlor.

Was that the reason she had chosen such thick wallpaper? Not just because she liked knotty pine? Not just because she was brassy and original and didn't give a damn, but to cover up the damage? Someone using a chisel couldn't have scarred the plaster much worse.

There were other reasons to start reading. The unknown woman had done Vera a huge favor by stripping off the first three layers, a job she would have found impossible on her own. This was a debt and a real one. Then, too, she was almost certainly the only other person to have read Beth's story, which formed a bond that couldn't be ignored.

She went back to the same method she had used with Beth, stripping bare the entire wall before allowing herself to read. With

Beth, she had the sensation of words pressing outward on the paper and helping, but this woman's words were gummier, they didn't want to let go of the paper that covered them, so she had to work twice as hard.

She was halfway through the first wall, on the point of taking her morning coffee break, when something surprising happened—surprising only in the fact it hadn't occurred sooner. It came from the radio, Jeannie's boom box, which had been her trusted companion all through work. The station played the same lulling French music as always, soothing precisely because she didn't understand a word, but then suddenly between songs the announcer said something she understood all too well.

"Iraq," he said, rolling the *r*. There were more words she couldn't understand, then two she could: "mort" and "soixante-quinze."

She felt betrayed, that was the strange thing. Mad at the radio, mad at Canada, mad at Quebec. She trusted them to stay neutral, and now here they were, deliberately targeting her, jabbing her with a needle, making fun of her—her desire for numbness, her vanity in thinking it was the easiest emotion in the world to achieve.

She turned it off, took it out to the hall, banished it from her hearing. She worked in silence, except for the steady scrapes and whispers made by the putty knife's blade. Too quiet, she thought at first. But then she had the first wall cleared, she was stepping back to read what was written there, and all became noisy very fast.

I can't tell a story like she can. Can't make you cry like she can wouldn't care to wouldn't know how. Oh plenty of tears alright a

lifetime's worth like everybody but most came on one terrible afternoon and that's buried in the past now a lot thicker than these
walls. Funny Dottie Peach who's always ready with a wisecrack
even a crude one even a mean one if somebody gets on my bad
side and someday if I'm not careful it's going to be Crazy Dottie
Peach who can't tell a story straight can't even start at the beginning. But if what goes round comes round what does it matter
where on the circle you start?

I can't tell a story like Beth can. I was born she says I was married she says I fell in love with another man. Joke's on her he
doesn't like girls. Damn her! I HATED it that she made me cry.
I thought she was going to run off with him isn't that what you
thought yourself? All that tragedy and why? He liked men. Okay
so it's deeper than that deep like the river those Nazi bastards
drowned him in while my story isn't deep at all but more like a
muddy puddle and telling it is like stirring with a stick until the
mud belches out words.

Can't tell a story like she can. The orphan business for starters.
I wish I HAD been an orphan. I remember reading Hansel and
Gretel when I was little wishing I had their evil stepmother for
my mother it would be such an improvement over who I did have.
Slapping me around when she was drunk and worse than that
from the man claiming to be my dad. He got a bright idea when
we bombed Nagasaki. He was working building ships on the coast
and he decided the future was in building atomic bombers on the
other coast and so we piled into our Chevy and headed West.
After about six hours we stopped here in the middle of nowhere.
They said let's take a pee break but when I came back outside

from the diner they were gone in a cloud of dust and I never saw either one of them again.

I was sixteen. I went back in the diner and asked for a job. I was Dorothea when I went in and Dottie by the time I tied the apron on since no one ever waitressed named Dorothea. My first customer sat hunched over the counter leering at me through the ketchup. Big man a lot older than me driving a logging truck idling outside.

"What'll you have?" I said all nervous and shy it being my first time.

"Steak?"

"Sure."

I wrote it down on my pad.

"Eggs?"

"You bet."

I wrote it down on my pad.

"Fuck?"

He said it loud making sure all the men in the place heard. What I should have done was take the coffee pot and pour some on his crotch. What I did do was stare right back at him and make my voice go flirty.

"I'd love to grandpa, but I'm menstruating."

The men in the booths howled and right there and then I got the reputation as being funny and tough and an egghead since I don't think any of them had ever heard that word out loud before. One of the youngest sitting sideways in the corner by the jukebox was dressed in uniform since he'd just been discharged. "He's Perry Peach," the other waitress giggled and I couldn't help be interested in a name like that. Not just Perry but Perry PEACH. He looked like Dana Andrews who was my favorite movie star with medals on his chest Silver Stars and the same waitress told me he'd come back from the Pacific with skulls as souvenirs. Once I got to know him he was always talking about Japs which was the worst thing he could say about somebody that he or she was a Jap. On our wedding night I flat out asked him about the skulls and he said sure he had them only he didn't want to frighten me so before the wedding he took them down to the river patted them on top for good luck and chucked them in.

I wasn't very pretty then but most men didn't lift their eyes much higher than my chest. I know Perry never did. He took a job with the highway crew which was considered practically an executive position up here ever since the Depression. It was enough to marry on and he didn't expect me to work. Bullshit on what I remember thinking. When you leave me what will I do starve? It's strange but I thought in those terms right from the start. He was the kind of man who's hot to trot before the wedding and Mr. Dullsville after. It was only a question of whether he would cheat on me and run off or whether I would cheat on him and run off and whether he would come after me and shoot me like he had all his Japs.

There was a community college starting up and they had a course for nursing aides. The classes were held in an old high school they were renovating and though I didn't know it at the time it was the school where Beth had gone on her milk train every morning. I got the best grades in class and one of my teachers said why stop at aide so I went back and got my RN. I guess

I'm the nurse type alright. I don't care much about strong people but weak ones break my heart.

So I walked the same halls that Beth walked maybe sat in the same desk. I even found a book of hers here in an upstairs closet called "Tennyson's Gareth and Lancelot and Elaine and the Passing of Arthur Idylls of the King" with her name written in front. That was in 1958 when we first moved in and I didn't think anything of it but chucked it in the trash. I was following her footsteps before I knew she even existed and when I started reading her story felt I understood her right away. Did she write the truth on the walls to get them arrested? You probably wonder about that too. Or did she write it down because she would have burst if she hadn't written it down????? Joke's on her either way because the next person who lived here papered right over HER wallpaper without stripping it off and the lazy bitch who lived here after that papered over THAT paper and it wasn't until I started stripping the layers just before Andy escaped home that anyone read it which means not until 1969 and now of course you've read it too so we're twins.

That was some summer that 69 summer. August especially. They had just made me assistant head nurse in cardiology but I told them I needed two weeks off first to take care of my garden and put up some wallpaper and celebrate my 41st birthday. The wallpaper was still the same drab stuff that was here when we bought the house from lazy Sally Bruckner and her even lazier husband. It holds the walls together I used to joke and I was always too busy bringing up the boys to bother about it one way or the other but now I could. I bought new paper at Real Value the best I could afford. Premium Pine one pattern was called and the other was Queen of Sheba. Brown would make the walls look warm on the cold side of the house and white would make the walls look cool on the warm side of the house and other than that I didn't give it much thought.

As for my garden it was dying right under my eyes. It hadn't rained since May and the weatherman claimed it was hotter here than in Texas and everyday I had to go outside and pull up another wilted flower or turn under another dead plant. The afternoon of my birthday I stood in what was left of my zinnia bed feeling more blue than I usually allow myself. I remember thinking something that hit me pretty hard though I tried making a joke of it. "I'm an abandoned woman," I told myself. "Dorothea Elizabeth Peach that's what you are, an ABANDONED WOMAN." Abandoned just like when my parents dumped me here and drove west into the sunset.

I always knew Perry would run out on me so that was no surprise. We had some good years together but that was when the boys were little and after that it was just him moving mechanically in the dark and me on my back trying to remember what it had once been like and between his hunching and heaving and my remembering and sobbing we sometimes managed to find love again but in the end it wasn't worth much just a note on the door one Christmas saying "Back later" which I knew meant "Back never."

The great love of his life was Danny and when Danny died there was nothing left to keep him here. Andy he never cared much for and didn't pay him much attention which was how everybody treated Andy myself included. But Danny! They were best pals from the time he was three months old and even when he was a toddler he wouldn't do anything unless Daddy did it too. Hunting fishing camping. I was all in favor of it and he was such a good student in school top of his class right through high school and his hair was the reddest anyone ever saw and he acted in plays and could do a hundred push-ups without puffing. Then his junior year he and Perry started watching Westerns together on TV and somehow that led them to getting involved with a "fast draw" club which was where you wore a six-gun on your hip like a cowboy and faced down someone else wearing their own revolver and saw who could yank their gun out of the holster first.

Danny was good at this like he was good at everything. Fast lickety-split fast. He wanted to add some tricks and learn how to twirl the pistol around on his finger but somehow the gun got loaded and somehow went off in his face and the next thing I know the phone is ringing in the hall and Tom Bottle our constable is screeching up out front to fetch me and we drive crazy fast to the gymnasium and what followed after were the worst hours of my life. I didn't know before that that I had a soul. All that fancy talk about souls and I used to listen skeptically because I never felt I had one but seeing Danny lying on the gym floor with his face covered by a cowboy bandanna taught me about souls and what it taught me was that souls exist alright but only to torture us.

That left Andy and then Andy left too. Drafted. There were hardly any young men left around here so who else could the draft board take? He once told me he wanted to be an astronaut but other than that he had no plans. He graduated high school on a Friday and Sunday he was on a train heading south to Fort Polk in Louisiana which the soldiers called Fort Puke. They had a mock Vietnamese village there called Tiger Land where troops got training before shipping out and the nearest town to the base was called Leesville which the soldiers called Diseaseville he wrote in his first letter home.

Andy was always in Danny's shadow and this made him quiet but he never gave anyone trouble but always went along with anyone and anything so following orders in the military wasn't going to be any problem just more of what he's good at. If teachers wanted him to study he studied and if friends wanted him to goof off and smoke dope he goofed off and smoked dope and if I wanted help raking the garden he was out there raking. But the funny thing is he never does any of those things with any kind of excitement or enthusiasm or interest he just puts his head down and does them and that is pretty much his entire philosophy of life. "She's a girl who can't say no," they say and they never apply it to a boy but they could apply it to Andy because whatever the situation is he always goes along.

So that was how things stood on my birthday. Only eight weeks ago but it seems eight years. "Don't torture yourself!" I remember thinking. I said it several times over as I walked past my wilted zinnias dusty petunias dead dahlias trying to make it my motto. DON'T TORTURE YOURSELF!!! And the truth is except for the pain over Danny which I know is permanent I didn't feel as lonely and abandoned as you might think. My dead flowers bothered me. The heat bothered me. And very faint and almost forgotten that other kind of heat the kind that comes with needing a man.

Okay so I'm crying on your shoulder. Let me cry. I needed a friend and still do for that matter. There's Mrs. LaBombard up the road and the nurses at work but not many besides that. YOU NEED ANOTHER FRIEND! I told myself and no sooner had I wished it than it happened.

She was delivered by bus that was the strange thing. Buses never go by here except when there's construction out of the highway and they use our road as a detour. A big Greyhound so silver and shiny it seemed to push away the heat stopping right by my house which surprised me considerably. The brakes squealed the door swung open and in the whoosh of cool air emerged a girl of about eighteen or nineteen. She turned around to take the knapsack the driver handed out to her which was the Boy Scout kind crammed so full it was impossible to understand why it didn't burst.

I knew from that first glimpse of her she was the prettiest girl who ever stepped foot in our town. She was barely five feet high and seemed even shorter because of the dress she wore which was soft and summery and clung to her in a way that was Kewpie doll perfect. Her hair was long down past her waist and straight as you can imagine not a curl in sight being the color you would get if you mixed buttercups with silk. Her face was round and full almost Russian I thought with eyes so big it was like she carried her own mirrors. Not mirrors she could stare into like so many vain girls but mirrors you could stare into yourself lit up by her warmth. She had that way about her. Freckles clustered around her nose just the right number and old-fashioned Valentine-shaped lips.

"Can I ask you a question?" she said in the softest voice imaginable. She set her knapsack down on the grass.

"You just did."

She turned and pointed. "How come those dark splashes appear over the hills and go away and come back again? Some look like maps and others look like butterflies. I watched them all the way along the highway. I never took my eyes off them."

It was a silly question a lot of her questions were silly and yet she always asked them with so much curiosity they didn't seem silly after all.

"Shadows from clouds," I said. "The hills are down here, the clouds are up there, and the sun is even higher so when they blow apart that's what happens."

She took that in very gravely hugged herself almost shivered. "It's the most beautiful sight I ever saw."

Probably nobody in three hundred years had stared at these hills without either hating them for blocking their way or appraising their potential to generate money. After all these centuries they had their first lover.

"Dottie Peach," I said sticking out my hand.

She smiled at the Peach part then hesitated. "My name is August," she said at last. "August," and she nodded emphatically up and down.

"Augusta?" I said.

"August."

Don't ask me how but I knew right away she had just invented it on the spot. New name new place new life. She put her hand on my shoulder for balance stooped down took off her city shoes and threw them as far as she could into the meadow so she was barefoot. She had taken the bus from New York she explained and now if I could help her with directions and maybe fill her canteen she would be on her way.

She had a map the kind the gas stations issue and she kneeled down to spread it open across her knapsack. "I need to find the Wooden Shoe," she said which was funny because the last place that would be plotted on any map was the Wooden Shoe.

I knew as much about the Wooden Shoe as anybody in town which means not a lot. Most people call it a camp because of the young people living there or because they use an abandoned logging camp as their headquarters. It's a huge piece of land they're squatting on maybe three thousand acres butting up against the border though it's all cut down and burned over and not much use to anybody. Dr. Goring went up there to stitch somebody's ankle after they'd nearly cut it off with an axe and he came back with some pretty strange tales. "It's a commune," he said making a face. "They wear beads. They eat straw. They're digging a moat." He swore he'd never go back up there again because they tried paying him in piglets.

The Wooden Shoe comes from a carved Dutch shoe hanging as a sign on the only road in. Now that people knew it was a commune and not some kind of fruity summer camp they became more suspicious since commune sounds like communist. The young people come into town to buy supplies and they look harmless enough dressed like pranksters and jesters with bows and ribbons and floppy hats. They operate a flatbed truck that barely bangs along and you can see it coming miles away with the exhaust it spews but it's decorated with the craziest brightest paint job you can imagine. "Psychedelic," Dr. Goring called it and we all thought that was a funny word that fit perfectly.

The being scared of them part started when Sheriff Bottle went up there on a tip and vowed never to return. "They don't pay me enough to deal with that shit!" he said and it was clear he was talking about drugs and guns and smuggling. It was hard to picture since the kids came to town so friendly and polite. The one thing people notice is that they're especially nice to old folks really courting them wooing them learning everything from them they possibly can. All the old-timers nobody cared about anymore were suddenly getting lots of attention and all the forgotten skills like sheep shearing and barn raising and cider making these Wooden Shoe kids were trying to learn because they HAD to learn if they were going to survive their first winter. NEVER TRUST ANYONE UNDER SEVENTY is their motto and they mean it.

They're all supposed to be equal up there brothers and sisters but you know as well as I do that never works out. Their leader the one they look to for every decision is a young man named Isaac Rosen who's about Andy's age but looks much older. You hear stories about Rosen most of which are probably made up but even so. There's one about his getting into a dispute with a Canadian smuggler over a busted drug deal and strangling him nearly dead and another's about getting in a fight with a black bear that tried breaking into their potato cellar and strangling it all the way dead. People say he's not only ruthless but smart and even has informers working for him in the Border Patrol and state police.

I've only seen him once or twice. He's rail thin razor thin thin as barbed wire or a very tough weed. His beard is the fuzzy kind they all wear only blonder and his mustache is like a whisper of contempt added across his lips. His eyes are the angriest I've ever seen on a man and I've seen plenty of angry eyes. A Civil War soldier is what he looks like one who fought on the losing side and doesn't intend to let that happen again.

Hunters in town went up there looking for deer and were met by Rosen and two of his disciples toting shotguns and steered right back out again. One of the hunters Ethan Whitcher had been going up there all his life so he tried to reason with them and what he got for an answer soon made its way around town. "We're an independent nation," Rosen told him. "You go back to America before we blow you all to hell."

This is where August this delicate barefoot doe-like girl wanted to go once she got off that bus. "Well, it's a long walk," I told her. "A good five or six miles until you come to the shoe. Let me give you a ride."

She didn't want a ride she wanted to walk which was important to her that she travel that last stretch on her own. She grabbed her pack and swung it around until most of the weight fell on her hip so it was like a baby she carried though a pretty hefty one. She walked past the house got caught up in the heat shimmering off the pavement and just before she dissolved completely I could make out the wavy remnants of her wafting toward the hills.

A week went by. It was still too hot to work on stripping the wallpaper but I went into town and bought some scrapers so I'd be ready once the heat broke. When I came home the mail had just been delivered with a letter from Andy which was a rare enough event. Things were still fine at Fort Puke. His company had finished basic now and were undergoing advanced infantry training attacking Tiger Land learning what it was like to fight in Vietnam. He volunteered for lots of jobs he said. Potato peeling ditch digging mosquito control. He couldn't stand it standing in ranks being asked for volunteers and no one raising his hand so he'd raise his. It just shot up he couldn't help it. Their instructor was named Sergeant Cobb who was tough but fair and you wouldn't want to get on his bad side but he had taken a fatherly interest in Andy so all in all things were fine. In their free time he was watching TV mostly so I didn't have to worry about him getting sick in Diseaseville.

No sooner had I finished reading this than I heard a soft whisking noise on the screen like a kitten scratching to get in. August! She had a happy smile on her face and was dressed in canvas overalls that made it seem like she had been working pretty hard though I noticed she had embroidered the floppy bottoms and tied on little bells.

"Come on in!" I said.

I asked if she was hungry and she said no but when I put out a plate of brownies she gobbled them up pretty fast then asked if I had any Coke. Maybe they didn't have enough food up there yet since growing season wasn't over or maybe she was used to so much sugar in the suburbs she needed to be weaned from it gradually.

During her walk she had woven a necklace of black-eyed Susans which she hung around my neck. We sat on the porch and I listened while she talked. It was mostly about her home down in New Jersey and how much she hated it though she spoke very soft. Everybody always so competitive so obsessed with money and status going to cocktail parties and bragging about what cars they drove voting Republican building ticky-tacky houses not caring about anything except the stock market meanwhile living the most destructive least sustainable way of living ever invented.

She rattled off her list then did something I thought was cute. She waved her hand toward the south and mouthed "Bye-bye" to it like a little girl.

I don't have a girl of my own to tell stories to or hear stories from so maybe that's what made her visits special. We never had those wars mothers and daughters go through when the mother wants the daughter to be like her and the daughter doesn't want to do that so there's war.

She said things were getting easier at the Shoe as they began forgetting the selfish every man for himself dog eat dog rat race world they had been brought up in. There was an aura of peace they could sense hovering right above them which was as real as the sunshine and the only way to let it descend was to create harmony among themselves and the only way to create harmony was to work and work digging the moat that was going to protect them from the outside world which was the term they gave to the independence they strove so hard to build except on Mondays which Rosen had decided were going to be devoted to meditation.

"Rosen, huh?" I grunted. "Sounds like he's the big cheese up there. Where's he hail from?"

"California. The desert part."

"Yeah? Well, does he ever talk about himself being the Messiah?"

She laughed with that. She thought my questions were hysterical.

"He has a new name," she told me. "We call him Granite now."

"Granite? Hard granite stone?"

She nodded. "Yes, only harder."

It was clear she admired him. He often hiked into Canada leading strangers who mostly kept their faces hidden and when he came back it was with more weed than they could possible smoke and this special kind of Canadian oatmeal everybody devoured. And there was good news now. Lilac her best friend the nicest girl the one everybody loved was pregnant and the baby could come at any time.

"Our baby," August called it. Everybody in the Shoe that's what they called it. Ours.

She drank two more Cokes before she left and I sent her away with some Oreos to munch on her long walk back. Next Thursday when she came I made sure I had chips and brownies and cupcakes and all the secret things she craved. A very sweet girl!!!

I told her that if they were going around gathering wisdom from the old folks then they better make sure to visit Mrs. LaBombard up the road. That's the old Hogg house which the LaBombards had bought after they left Quebec during the Depression and the reason they left Quebec was because Edgard LaBombard was an atheist and communist and every other radical thing you can be up there and since the Catholic church was in charge of relief he either had to bring his family across the line or starve.

He died a long time ago but Therese LaBombard is pushing a hundred. "I came to America in Nineteen Tirty-Tree with my tirteen children and voted for Roosevelt tree times," she likes to say and if you smile at what she does to English she'll switch right over to French.

She's the best cook I know especially with potatoes and game which is why I told August to look her up. "Extended" they say about recipes up here and no one can extend a recipe like Therese can. Nowadays they call french fries with gravy "poutines" but she sneers at that and makes poutines the old way boiling potatoes in cheesecloth and drenching them in maple syrup. Tourtier and chicken tricot and a hundred dishes made from turnips. There's always something baking at Therese LaBombard's!

Much later after everything that happened happened and things grew quiet again and I finally got the wallpaper stripped off I went over to her place with a question.

"My house, Therese."

We were rocking on her porch but now she stopped and squinted at me over the black plastic glasses that were always sliding down her nose.

"Oui?"

"The Bruckners owned it before us."

She made a face. "Lazy people. Ate from cans."

"And before them?"

"Howards. Here when we moved in. Nineteen Tirty-tree."

"Before them?"

I could see her thinking looking out toward the hills. She wasn't used to being asked something about the past she couldn't answer.

"Don't know," she said with a despairing shrug.

"A family named Steen? The rich people in town? A young woman named Beth? Any of those ring a bell?"

Therese wasn't a quitter not when it involved figuring out connections so I believe my questions tortured her considerably. I felt guilty for asking but there was no other person in town who might remember.

When she shook her head I tried a different tack. "Did you ever hear stories about a teacher who was drowned in the river?"

"A teacher? In the river?" She clasped her hands to her cheeks. "Mon Dieu!"

"Thank you, Therese. Merci beaucoup. And don't forget about those young people I mentioned. You teach them about turnips and they'll be grateful."

I'm skipping you around now and we need to move summer back the other way to eight days after August's second visit. The heat broke that afternoon. A thunderstorm boomed down from Canada and within the space of ten minutes the temperature dropped twenty degrees. It got dark as early as it does in winter so by five I could hardly grope my way over to switch on the lights. There was a bang on the door that made me jump and then whoever it was ran around to the back and started hammering there even louder.

It was August plus a girl with frizzy hair and terrible acne and a skinny young man wearing a green poncho and hip boots. August's face was too open and soft to express alarm but there was definitely anxiety there and her hair was flattened to her cheeks from the rain. "We need your help," she said reaching for my arm. It was because I'm a nurse and they didn't know anybody else who would come.

They had brought the truck down and the rain made its psychedelic paint even more psychedelic like it was sloshing crazily back and forth along the sides. I grabbed my boots and they hoisted me up on back. The ride into the hills was the wildest I've ever been on since on their way down to fetch me they had blown out two tires and the young man named Gabriel drove on the rims. Add to that the rain wind thunder and having to swerve around downed trees and ducking under branches so as not to get swept off and the two girls clutching at me and vampire bats yo-yoing up and down making the girls scream and all in all it was a trip to remember.

It took an hour to get to the Shoe sign which the wind had snapped so the toe stuck in the mud. The rain wasn't quite as bad here and there was enough light in the sky to see the land was all blasted and ruined with nothing but jagged tree stumps and huge piles of slash. Geezus I said to myself. What A-bomb fell here? A tractor was mired off to the side of the road near a trench wide enough to make me wonder whether they were digging a moat after all. There were pennants or banners stretched across the trees and then when we got to the main building there was a flag with vertical bands I had my suspicions might be Vietnam's and I don't mean the South part either.

August tugged me toward the door but first I told Gabriel to get some tires on the truck and get them on quick in case we had to go fetch a doctor. I knew now it was Lilac I had been called for because there's a smell that comes during childbirth that maybe only a mother can catch or a nurse but it's got urine in it and blood and sweat and something sweeter that's hard to describe but was waiting for me the moment I went in.

This had once been a logging camp and you could still see scars on the floor from hobnailed boots. The homemade table and chairs had been shoved against the wall to make room for a bed lit by kerosene lamps hanging down from the rafters. Lilac lay on a mattress where the beams converged and judging by the way she rolled and heaved she was well along. She was a little slip of a girl who seemed even smaller with the enormous thing that was try-ing to happen just down from her middle. I went right over and knelt by the table and told her my name and said I was there to help things along and she nodded in gratitude though I don't think she was aware of much now except the force that had hold of her which had to be bewildering compared to what puny forc-es she could muster against it. She took my hand and pressed it hard to her breast then moved it to her mouth found a finger and started desperately sucking. For comfort I suppose. I let her suck all she wanted.

We weren't exactly alone with this. The other commune mem-bers squatted on their heels against the wall watching so it was like summer camp after all and this was an initiation ceremony they were required to attend. My first instinct was to shoo them all away but then I realized Lilac was drawing strength from hav-ing them near. "Our baby" August called it and maybe they were helping by just being there tightening their pelvises in sympathy the girls or feeling their penises shrivel in guilt the boys. There was one big girl with thick pigtails who looked serene as a Viking princess and I delegated her to keep mopping Lilac's brow while I concentrated on what was happening lower down.

What was happening lower down looked normal enough to me though naturally it scared them especially with her moans which were awfully LOUD. I didn't think we'd need to send to town for my doctor friend but could see it through ourselves. It wasn't even a nurse they especially needed. What they needed and needed badly was an adult.

Two adults. For standing against the wall rocking slowly back and forth on heels was Rosen or Granite or whatever he wanted to be called. A lot of men intimidate you with their size and brawn but he was one of those rarer ones who impress you by their thinness like they're showing you they don't need much from life and because they don't need much from life they're a hell of a lot tougher than you are. He had on ragged work pants a red flannel shirt taut suspenders and looked like he had stepped into that room from 1885. He stroked his blonde beard while he rocked but never smiled never came close to smiling. Granite is a good name for him since his skin is steel gray with albino veins and you know if you touched him touched him anywhere nothing would flinch.

He was the one I glanced at whenever I needed something. Towels hot water compresses rubbing alcohol swabs. I only had to nod and he knew instinctively what I wanted and went to fetch it. I liked him for that hard as he was. And for all the talk about it being "our" baby I knew from the intent way he stared that the baby was his.

Lilac's labor lasted most of the night but there were no surprises other than how a little thing like her could howl so loud and so long. I didn't need to do much until the baby began crowning than I started in massaging since I wanted it to be positioned just right. Maybe that helped because toward the end Lilac became much quieter. The last hour was rough even so. I'm just as glad a doctor wasn't there because he would have gotten impatient and reached for the forceps but I waited and in the end hardly needed to do anything but tie off the cord. The Viking girl turned out to be named Kit and she did a good job cleaning the baby and wrapping him and handing him to Lilac who once her exhaustion wore off and her disbelief smiled so beautifully it made me sob.

"What's his name?" I said slipping open the blanket enough to admire him.

"Luddy," she said.

I didn't get it.

"Muddy?"

"Luddy."

"Cuddy?"

"Luddy."

"Perfect name," I said. I never heard of it before.

I'm making myself out to sound like an expert but that was the first birth I'd ever been at where I wasn't the one doing the pushing and moaning. I was never frightened though and that's because I drew strength from the eager hopeful way those young people stared. I don't know if any of them is an artist but you could paint a pretty good picture if you'd been watching that night. The rain streaming down the windows and the kerosene lamp beaming off the pink hill of Lilac's belly and luna moths beating their wings against the screens trying to get in and the warmth of the wood-stove on our backs and the girls twirling their necklaces like rosary beads and the boys smoking weed and Granite over there in his corner holding us all together by the fearless way he stared. I looked over once and saw twin gold dots toward the bottom of the window felt it was raccoons come to watch or porcupines or bob-cats and sensed at their back the wild forest land that surrounded us lonely beyond lonely forgotten beyond forgotten hardly even part of America at all and yet right there in the center pressing it back bawling its head off this gift of new life.

It was dawn the sun was burning the dew off the windows before I felt sure enough about things to leave. Granite walked me out to the truck and before we got there he grabbed one of his men by the shoulders and pointed to the old stable they used as their barn.

I was way ahead of him.

"Nope, I don't want any piglets," I said. "This was for free."

That seemed to annoy him. He didn't like being beholden to anybody. It would be better if I liked pigs.

"Nope," I said again. "Don't want any lambs either or honey or berries or dope. Had some fun here, thanks go to you."

August rode back with me on the truck and when we got to my house she didn't want to let me go.

"Out with it," I said. I could see those soft round eyes holding something in.

"Why does it have to be torture?"

I said what any woman would say.

"Because it always is, always has been, always will be."

This didn't seem to satisfy her and I know it didn't satisfy me and probably sounds easy and smug to you. But I guess that's what they wanted me to say why I was brought up there what my role in all this was. To tell them the miracle we witnessed wasn't so special after all but the most natural thing in the world.

The words looked tattooed, she had pressed so hard on the skin of plaster. Every fifth or sixth sentence ended with gouges instead of periods and Vera finally understood these were places where the points of her pens must have snapped, just like the lead of pencils. What kind of woman writes so hard the pen breaks? What kind of woman would use three colors of ink and change colors, it sometimes seemed, almost every word? And how many cartons of pens must she have bought, to be so extravagant?

At first the writing extended all the way across the wall, but she must have realized she would never fit in everything she had to say, because she suddenly switched to relatively neat and ordered paragraphs similar to Beth's. Maybe it was the strain of this that made the pens snap—she didn't like margins, borders, indents, rules.

Reading Beth, Vera's head had remained steady and intent, a platform for her attention to rest on, but reading Dottie, trying to follow her swoops and splashes, her head kept swaying, so the words seemed to come through the muscles of her neck. The childbirth business came that way—by the time she finished reading she was massaging her shoulders trying to press out the kinks. Having Cassie had been ridiculously easy, to the point she was even somewhat disappointed that she hadn't had the chance to prove her determination and courage.

"Don't you worry about that," the maternity nurse told her. "The ones that cause no trouble now torture you plenty later."

Torture. Maybe it was a nurse word. Dottie had used it four times and each time it was as if she had reached her hand out from the wall and slapped Vera across the face. She had probably jotted it down without a moment's thought, hyperbole but who cared, never worrying about how someone might react, that unknown someone who forty years later would be reading what she wrote.

Badly—how else could she react? Extravagantly. Wildly. She could have cursed reading the word the first time and she could have shouted the second time and the third time she could have screamed and even that wouldn't have been commensurate with what she felt. The word had slapped her, then fallen off the plaster right smack into her lap, with those spiky *t*'s and sordid *r*'s and the dirty vowels that served as their glue.

She went out to the kitchen and fixed herself supper to get away from it. She swept the wallpaper scraps off the floor and burned them outside to get away from it. She stood naked under the hose. But her little cleansing ceremonies didn't work, nothing worked, and so she went the other way, deliberately thought of the word constantly, saying it over and over to herself until it was nonsense.

Torture. Torture. Torture. Torture. That old childhood trick, like deliberately spinning yourself around and around on the grass until you got dizzy. Torture. Torture. Torture. Torture. Torture.

That was better, it was beginning to blur now—she turned the sewing room lamp off and went upstairs to the bedroom. Torture. Torture. Torture. Torture. Torture. Torture. Torture. She said it so many times it became automatic, her imagination kept it up in her sleep. Torture became torch-her became tore-her became toss-her became touch-her—and touch-her had never hurt any-one. When she woke up in the morning, went downstairs, ate breakfast, picked up her tools and began stripping, determined to finish the room in one final go, the word hardly meant anything, Dottie could use it all she wanted, it was nothing but a blur of ugly syllables that hardly tortured her at all.

Two days later I discovered Beth's writing with the very first strip I peeled off the wall in the TV room which I guess had been her parlor but we had put the TV in there when we first bought the house and it's

been there ever since up on a shelf along with all my women's maga-
zines and Danny's first buck or at least its antlers. There was a fold-
out couch I kept meaning to replace and a coffee table with a
checkerboard built into the top where Danny always used to beat
Andy and Andy never seemed to mind. Since becoming an abandoned woman I didn't see any reason to keep it tidy so it was the
room that needed working on the most.

I wasn't as surprised by the writing as you might think. Ever
since we moved here I had sensed somebody else in the house like
a restless presence that couldn't rest. Ghosts you're thinking and
you're probably laughing. But I never thought ghosts I thought
well some poor soul once lived here who had a hard time and the
echo of that is still bouncing off the walls. Peeling back that first
strip you know what I thought? THERE YOU ARE!!! just like
in hide and go seek. Even then I was slow on the uptake. I thought
it was a recipe she had jotted down on the wall while she was
papering or a calculation about how many rolls she needed or
some simple sort of reminder.

If I stripped off more paper I would have discovered what it
really hid but just then I heard a noise outside like a giant blender
crushing ice. I felt like I'd been caught doing something secret so
I reached up as high as I could and tucked the edge of that first
strip back under the molding and patted it down so the writing
was hidden again and only then went outside.

A big Greyhound bus was pulling over to the side of the road
ANOTHER BUS so it seemed like my place had suddenly become Grand Central Station. The driver climbed down muttering
to himself and right behind him of all people came Andy! "Lend
a hand?" the driver asked and Andy nodded. He gave me a little

wave and followed the driver around to the back of the bus and the next thing I knew the two of them were under there hammering away at a pipe that had bounced loose on one of our potholes. When they scooted back out again Andy's uniform was covered in mustard-colored grease which made him look like a hot dog after crawling through a bun. The driver climbed inside then threw a duffel bag down to him and snapped off a salute.

"Enjoy your leave, soldier! When you get over there give 'em hell for me!"

That eased the shock since at least I knew now it was leave that had brought him home. He hadn't said anything in his last letter but he was never one to say. He leaned over and kissed me on the forehead like he'd only been gone a few hours and followed me over to the porch. I think he would have continued right straight to the TV room but I wasn't going to let him do that at least not right away.

"Home sweet home," I said sort of prompting him.

He looked around and nodded. "Home sweet home."

"So, you got a leave?"

"Yeah."

"Regular?"

"Embarkation."

"You're going?"

"Nam."

"How long is your leave?"

"Thursday."

"And you ship out?"

"Monday."

"I thought it might be Germany."

"Nope."

That's pretty much how our conversation went the two of us circling around each other on the porch like Cassius Clay and Sonny Liston me jabbing him ducking.

"Well come on in, come on in! Take your shirt or tunic or whatever it's called off and I'll put it in the wash."

You need to be careful with Andy since if you tell him something he'll do it. Right there on the porch he started stripping off his uniform! That made me laugh. Same old Andy! But the truth is he looked different than when he left not skinny and hard like you would think after basic training but thicker and puffier especially around the middle. His hair was pushed straight back in a crew cut and his acne was just as tomato red as ever and his eyes still had that meekness that used to irritate his dad and the dimple under his lip still reminded me of Kirk Douglas but what surprised me most was that over his belt hung the beginning of a paunch. I couldn't help sticking out my hand and patting it as sort of a question.

"Good chow," he said. "The cooks are pals of mine and I can never say no when they offer me seconds."

That's all I could get out of him about army life. He went up to his room and when he came back he had on the white t-shirt and khaki work pants that had always been his favorite clothes. I asked if he was thirsty but he said not particularly and went right over to the TV room and plopped himself down on the couch. One of his favorite shows was on which turned out to be a soap opera and he told me who all the characters were and what rotten things they were doing to each other. Just by luck I had chicken cutlets in the ice box which had always been his favorite and I fixed them with red potatoes and corn on the cob and maple biscuits and brought it to him on his old Donald Duck tray and when he saw what it was I got the first real smile I'd seen yet.

I sat down on our beanbag chair so he was in between me and the TV screen and though I pretended to watch it what I mostly did was watch him. Part of what I felt was what any mom would feel if her boy was going off to war proud and apprehensive but after that it got more complicated. Vietnam sat off in this numb zone that had something to do with television and something to do with politics and since I never had time for either of those things it could have been Mars they were talking about. No one in town had ever been sent there. It would have worried me more if he had been going to Germany to face all those Russian missiles and tanks.

Loving Danny losing Danny had worn me out I'm not ashamed to admit that. Both before and after his brother's death Andy was just THERE he wasn't the kind of boy you worried about and so it was hard to worry about him now. He had his arm hooked over the back of the couch to keep from sliding off onto the carpet but he kept inching lower and lower anyway and it was pretty funny how limp he became how slack. I thought to myself well that's Andy for better or worse. That's Andy and he's all I have left in the world and I love him more than I ever thought.

"This next one's my favorite," he said and just like that he was sitting ramrod straight on the couch. "Is it nine yet?"

He didn't look like he could bear waiting. He patted the couch made a space for me and once the program came on talked a mile a minute telling me what it was about.

"The Man from Uncle," he said. "They're good guys and what's funny is one of them is a Russian and yet they work together stamping out world crime. See? There he is! Ilya Kuriagin. Uncle is the agency they work for. Here's the other one, Napoleon Solo. They're getting their assignment, hold on to your hat!"

He was still watching TV when I went to bed and he may have been there all night because when I got up in the morning he was back on the couch though now he wore a black t-shirt not a white one. If that's how he wanted to relax during his leave it was fine by me though later in the morning I asked him to help me gather blueberries and of course he hopped right up. He was good at picking he could hold cupfuls in his hands but I was pretty good myself so we soon started a competition to see who could fill their bucket up first.

He took a shower after that went back to the TV. About four I heard somebody at the front door. August! I hadn't seen her since Lilac's baby and as we stood on the porch she filled me in on the news. They had cleared brush for a field. Their berries were spectacular. There was a new calf. Luddy was adorable. Granite had come back from Canada with the sweetest weed yet.

"That's wonderful," I told her. "But you must be tired from your walk. Come inside with me there's a little surprise."

I led her down the hall to the TV room but all there was of Andy was an empty depression in the couch. "Wait here," I told her and went out to the kitchen then up to his room but there was no sign of him. That confused me but since I hadn't told August about him yet I took her back outside. I'd been meaning to intro-duce her to Therese LaBombard and I figured now was as good a time as any and when I walked her up there the two of them immediately hit it off. August had learned French at private school and Therese spoke Quebecois but they managed to understand each other all right and Mrs. L. gave her a blueberry ketchup recipe that had been in her family for years.

I walked August a little way in toward the hills and stood watching until she was out of sight. When I went back into the TV room Andy sat slumped on the couch.

"Where'd you disappear to?" I said. I figured he was shy with so pretty a girl.

"I didn't disappear anywhere, Mom. I've been right here all afternoon."

That was a lie but for the life of me I couldn't figure out why he would bother. But that was the last day of my vacation and I didn't want to ruin it by arguing. I made meatloaf for dinner and we watched TV for a while and then I asked him to go for a walk with me to watch the sunset and he gave me a nice hug before I went up to bed.

"I'm really glad to have you here," I told him.

"Me, too," he said softly. "Really happy."

I always leave for work before the sun comes up but I left a note saying that maybe later we could go for a swim in the stream or drive into town for ice cream. At the hospital things were crazy busy mostly the usual confusion that comes when you've been gone on vacation but then a patient coded in the afternoon and no one could get an IV started on this retired railroad man and his family got hysterical and Tina Holbrook came up to our floor and started yelling at me for messing up her overtime schedule. As if that wasn't enough one of our orderlies Tom Titus who had spent the last eight years leering at me every time I came in range slunk up to me by the desk as I was getting ready to go home.

"You're gorgeous," he said which was his usual opening line.

"Not now, Tom."

"Fuck you then." He pointed toward the lounge at the end of the hall. "This bald farty guy wants to talk to you."

The good thing was that Tom put me in a bad mood. I walked down the hall determined not to take shit from anyone. The bald guy resembled a gangster with a forehead of cement and jowls that looked stuffed with fishing sinkers so I wasn't surprised when he waved a card in my face and announced he was a cop.

"Federal Bureau of Investigation," he said with a smirk.

He had a Boston accent and his cheek was scarred with a birthmark that looked like a slab of bubble gum plastered across the side of his nose. FBI? I felt like saying. You look like the kind of crook the FBI is supposed to hunt down. But I didn't say that.

"Bullshit," I said.

He seemed used to that.

"When's the last time you saw your son?" he demanded.

"Danny? 1964. He shot himself playing cowboy."

The agent looked down at his clipboard.

"Andrew Peach."

I'd held on to my attitude until then which was all about laughing him off but the moment he said Andy's name everything changed so fast it was like one of our nurses had given me a hypodermic that pumped wariness and caution right straight into my heart.

"Three months ago when he left for basic. Why? There's nothing wrong with him is there officer?"

The agent moved his tongue around so it was like he was licking the bubble gum from inside.

"He went on embarkation leave three weeks ago and hasn't reported back since. His unit shipped out last Tuesday for Vietnam. It was AWOL before that but now it's desertion."

"Missed the plane? He can catch another one, you must have plenty."

"Desertion means fifteen years in the stockade. Aiding and abetting him means five years in a federal penitentiary, a $25,000 fine, plus we take your house. I'll ask you again, Mrs. Peach. Have you seen your son or do you know where he might be hiding?"

"You must be mistaken, officer. Andy loves the army, he was looking forward to going overseas. He's the easiest boy in the world to get along with."

"You haven't seen him? Haven't gotten a phone call? Gotten a letter?"

"I have no idea where he is."

"I hope that's veracious. My men are searching your house this very minute."

My heart jumped with that and I made a fluttering gesture with my hand like Scarlett O'Hara about to faint. The agent decided he had me just where he wanted. He warned me again about the penalties for desertion then went on to say that if Andy turned himself in or reported to Fort Polk all would be forgiven but he only had twenty-four hours and past that anything might happen since there was a war on even though plenty of people pretended there wasn't. He finished by giving me his business card telling me he'd be in touch and then as he grabbed his fedora he asked a final question that seemed the most random and pointless of all.

"How far is Canada from here, Mrs. Peach?"

"Ten miles. You going sightseeing?"

He grimaced enough that his jowls jiggled but he didn't answer me or at least not directly.

"Canucks," he said. "Fucking animals."

The drive home was torture. I was sure some mistake had been made though I couldn't understand what the mistake was or how I could fix it and this drove me crazy plus I expected to see Andy being led from the house in chains. It's normally a twenty-minute drive but I did it in ten. Too fast too obvious so I slowed down and drove past the house to make sure I wasn't being followed. Things seemed peaceful enough and when I got to the porch and heard the TV blaring I wanted to cry in relief.

Andy sat slumped on the couch staring at one of his soap operas and didn't realize I was there until I stepped in front of the screen and turned it off.

"Hey," he said in gentle protest.

I didn't waste any time.

"When did they come?"

He looked sleepy like I had interrupted his nap and rubbed his eyes like the sandman had him.

"Hour ago."

"Where did you hide?"

"Never had to. They didn't come here. They drove up the road to Mrs. LaBombard's. Three cars full. I heard her shouting and that's how I knew they were there."

"They went to the wrong house?"

"I'll say. She was shouting at them in French and waving a broom around. They didn't look happy and so they drove off."

I can't tell you how calmly he said this like all the excitement had nothing to do with him.

"Explain," I said sitting down on the couch next to him.

Home three days and already the brushy tips of his crewcut were beginning to soften and curl over and he sat there trying to stroke them flat. He had some nasal problems when he was little which makes it seem like he sighs whenever he takes a deep breath and that's what I got now one of his deepest most reluctant sighs.

"We were due to ship out from San Diego and they said if we wanted to spend our five days of embarkation leave there it was okay we could join the unit at the air base once our time was up."

He folded his hands together and smiled.

"That's it?"

"Well, a bunch of us thought that would be fun so we went to the Greyhound station."

"And?"

"We had to wait at the lunch counter for the next bus west. I got talking to this discharged private who had just gotten back from Nam. He was going home to Nashville and he was complaining about how long a trip it was and it was boring without anybody to talk to and if I had nothing better to do why didn't I come along with him and when we got there he could show me the sights."

"So instead of San Diego you went to Nashville?"

"Didn't want to hurt his feelings. He had hundreds of stories about things he'd seen while he was fighting over there. You know. Not so nice things. But when we stopped in Little Rock he got talking to this hooker and didn't get back on the bus so I changed my ticket and headed for Knoxville instead."

"Knoxville? Why Knoxville?"

Andy shrugged. "Always liked the sound of it." He rapped his hand against the wall. "Knock knock who's there?"

"You stayed?"

"Couple of days."

"Doing?"

"Thinking about things."

"What things?"

"Met this girl and she was going to Atlanta and she asked me to go along and I said sure why not. I was AWOL by then anyway. It was pretty hot in Atlanta and I couldn't get cool no matter what I did and her boyfriend showed up so that's when I began thinking about heading home."

"That doesn't explain anything, Andy." I leaned toward him made sure he looked right into my eyes so his attention wouldn't wander to the blank TV screen. "The FBI man said you're not just AWOL you're deserting. You missed the plane to Vietnam. He said that's serious, you could go to prison. That's why I'm telling you that doesn't explain anything, what you just said."

He mumbled something.

"What?"

"I didn't really feel like it."

"Feel like what?"

"Going over there."

"To Vietnam?"

He put his hand on his chin used it to lever his head up and down in a heavy nod.

"You didn't feel like it?"

"Nah, not really."

"That's why you didn't go?"

"Don't really want to."

Already I was lost.

"Don't want to what?"

"Go over there."

"Because?"

"I'm not in the mood."

"Not in the mood?"

"Yeah, you know."

"The mood?"

"To kill anyone."

It staggered me not so much what he said but the lazy way he said it. By now I was agitated enough for both of us but I tried keeping my voice calm.

"Look, Andy. This G-man was pretty reasonable. You can go back he said, no questions asked. You can get on a plane and join up with your unit and all will be forgiven."

He shrugged. "I'm not really in the mood."

"You trained with these boys, they're counting on you. Didn't you train with them?"

"Tigerland. I did Tigerland with them."

"You don't want to put that experience to work, all that team-work?"

It didn't sound like me talking it sounded like the FBI bastard talking through me but what else could I do? He didn't answer right away seemed to think about it but then ended up saying exactly the same thing.

"Don't really feel like it."

I tried again this time desperately.

"Your father served in the Pacific. Your grandfather built destroyers. They answered their country's call."

Andy smiled.

Something occurred to me. "It wasn't any peace marchers talking to you messing up your head was it?"

"You mean draft dodgers?" He turned his finger up. "We hate them."

"But you believe in peace?"

He struggled with that for a minute or two.

"Nah, not particularly. It's just that I'm not in the mood."

I'm not sure how long I tried reasoning with him but it was dark by the time I quit. I tried scaring him about what would happen if he didn't go tried convincing him he owed it to his buddies brought out every argument I could think of and we always circled back to the same point.

"No," I said putting up my hand. "I know what you're going to say. But don't you think your mood could change?"

Instead of answering he went over to the TV squatted found the knob turned it on.

That left me with only one thing to say.

"It's just macaroni and cheese tonight, is that okay?"

"Thanks, Mom. You bet. You're the greatest."

I walked around the house before bed convinced there was a G-man lurking behind every bush. To calm myself down I tried remembering how Andy was as a little boy but that was difficult because the peculiar thing about Andy is that memories don't stick to him. I have a thousand memories of Danny all I have to do is close my eyes and they flood back. With Andy it's harder they seem to burrow shyly into the past and you really have to tug to bring them out.

But one finally came. He was five or six. Danny's father had taken him off on a hunting trip so it was just Andy and me in the house. He had a terrible accident only boys can have zipping his jeans up on the loose skin of his penis so he cried and cried and cried. I got things straightened away but then much later when I was sewing I heard his voice calling soft and despairingly from his room.

"Mommy? Am I going to die?"

That was my Andy memory and it broke the logjam so in the course of the night I found dozens of others I thought were lost. When I finally did fall asleep something happened that had nothing to do with thinking. I went to bed fretting and woke up absolutely convinced what I had to do.

Hide him. I had to hide him. I lost my first son and there's nothing worse a mother can say and my instincts were shriveled up for a long time after that but the pressure over Andy was good for them they had healed during the night or started to heal. I needed to trust how I felt needed to make sure the bastards wouldn't get him and if they did it would be over my dead body and so sure was I of this so certain that it didn't seem like an exaggeration but the literal truth.

OVER MY DEAD BODY I told myself. It was amazing how calm this made me feel.

Something else was working on me. I'd messed up the marriage business and been a failure with Danny and never accomplished very much outside work but here life was offering me one more test and I couldn't fail again.

"So," I said when he came downstairs for breakfast. "Still don't feel like killing anybody?"

He stirred his eggs around with his fork. "Not really in the mood."

"Then finish eating and follow me."

His bedroom has a closet under the eaves which runs all the way along the top floor of the house so it must be thirty feet long. Only the first six feet looks like a closet but if you push aside the rack of clothes and box of shoes it keeps going like a tunnel. Danny and Andy loved hiding in there as kids. The slanting wall of the closet stops a foot short of the outside wall of the house. There's a gap and if you push the insulation aside and crawl through you come out onto the rafters over the mudroom.

"Get some plywood from the barn," I told Andy. "We'll make a platform just big enough for you to stretch out on."

He hadn't been so enthusiastic about anything since he'd been home and before the morning was over we had the hiding place swept out and organized so it was like making a tree house or cave. We stocked it too. Flashlight flyswatter canteen blankets pillows cupcakes chips. Andy was disappointed he couldn't drag the TV in but other than that he seemed pleased. Good thing too because no sooner had we finished than somebody began knocking on the door downstairs.

It was a Western Union telegram boy or that's what he pretended to be. He looked about sixty and between that and my never having gotten a telegram in my life I was immediately suspicious.

"Telegram for Andrew Peach," he said. I still had my robe on and I saw him blushing but it wasn't my breasts that were doing it to him but the shame and embarrassment of having to lie.

"Telegram?" I said all innocent. "Well you've come to the wrong place, sonny. He's down in Diseaseville in the army."

The next day a UPS man knocked on the door claiming he had a package for Andy and I told him the same thing. These were like fire drills and Andy learned to scoot into the hiding place pretty quick. August came that afternoon on her weekly visit and it was hard for me since she was so open and loving and yet I couldn't even begin to tell her what was happening or how I felt. I kept her outside mostly but then we went into the kitchen and I made her some whoopie pies to take back to the Shoe. She was excited because they had traded for their first heifer and by winter hoped to have a bull if they could find a farmer willing to let one go. She ate her pies and I thought maybe her expression was a little more curious and questioning than usual but that was probably just me.

The state police came on Tuesday. I had called in sick for two days but couldn't do that anymore and I'd left a note for Andy and was on my way out to the car when three cruisers pulled up to the house. I knew all of them either because they lived in town or because I saw them at the hospital when they brought victims in after car wrecks.

"Mrs. Peach?" Robbie Silver said acting formal and stiff. I've known him since he was seven. "We have a warrant to search for your son."

They could have found him if they really wanted to but they not only knew me from way back when they knew Andy from way back when and if you knew Andy it was impossible to believe he could do anything so energetic as deserting. I was smart enough to ask if they wanted coffee and when I went into the kitchen I slipped the note I'd left Andy into the trash. Gus Lombardo rummaged through the bedroom closet but only got as far as the box of shoes and came back out holding his nose.

At least Robbie had the decency to act ashamed. "I'm sorry about this, Dottie."

"It's a funny thing," I said.

"Funny?"

"I never figured you for Gestapo."

Once they left I waited to make sure they wouldn't double right back. "Andy?" I called into the closet. After a few seconds seemingly a hundred miles away he called back.

"I'm happy, Mom."

"Well come on out, they're gone now."

"I think I'll stay in here for a while."

"Come on out, Andy. There's nothing to worry about."

The curtain made by his old baseball shirt and Boy Scout uniform parted and there he was stooping under the rod acting embarrassed trying to hide something around behind him and it was a few seconds before I realized what he was hiding was a dark stain on the seat of his pants.

I'd felt protective before this but it was nothing compared to what I felt now. "It's hot in there, you go and take a shower and I'll get lunch ready," I said trying to keep my voice calm. Never in my life had I felt pity like that or determination. All that talk about war with Russia made Perry stock the house with guns and while I got rid of most of them after he left there was a shotgun I saved to scare crows off my garden and what's more I knew how to use it. While Andy showered I went and found it and put it under my bed. Guns had taken my first son they could damn well protect my second.

There was a lull of three or four days where no one bothered us. I pulled Andy away from the TV long enough to discuss his plans though that was a joke because neither of us could come up with any. What I wanted was for the war to end and everybody be forgiven but one glance at the news at night threw cold water on that. I knew draft dodgers were safe if they got to Canada and I was guessing that meant deserters too but even though the border was just ten miles away it didn't seem like a real possibility.

Canada could have been Poland or Africa for all we knew about it. The high school basketball team sometimes went up there for games and there were plenty of Frenchies in town and people with bad teeth drove there for cheap dentists but except for bootleggers in the old days and drug smuggling now it was hard to think of any connections with Canada at all. There was only one road leading up there only one border crossing and it was sure to be watched. You could bushwhack through the woods and swamps but Andy was never what you would call outdoorsy and sent on his own he would probably lose his way and starve.

On Saturday we felt confident enough that he came outside and helped me work in the garden through a perfect August afternoon. We talked about taking a swim in the stream to cool off but then suddenly a hoarse gritty stirring in the air caught my attention and my sixth sense kicked in and putting my finger to my lips I shooed him inside.

I went around to the porch and for the third time that summer had a Greyhound bus squeal to a stop in front of my house.

The driver got out a different one than last time but just as polite and put down his stool with a little flourish and even whisked it off. The passenger who climbed down bowed and slapped him on the back so it was obvious that in the course of the bus ride they had become great pals.

There's no use pretending. What struck me first about the passenger was his blackness and his blackness almost knocked me down. In two hundred years probably not a single negro had ever set foot in town since we never had slaves and there are no cities nearby and we don't get tourists even white ones. And his blackness was black there was no brown. Between that and his being so well dressed in a sports jacket that was a little tight on him and a skinny white tie and a straw fedora with a madras band my first reaction was that this was one of those civil rights campaigners come to integrate us.

Big mistake. No civil rights worker had a waist like his which was small as a ballerina's or shoulders which were like a lumberjack's or held that ramrod posture and made it seem perfectly natural and at ease.

He carried no bag and the bus drove off without the driver tossing one down. He looked at the hills just like August had and like August seemed stunned by their beauty. He finally saw me and stared for a long time and I don't want to say he mentally stripped off my clothes because that's going to make it seem like all I think black men do is go around lusting after white women's bodies but that's what he did he mentally stripped me and then was polite enough to soften his expression and let me get dressed.

First words out of his mouth. "Any bears up here? Looks like evil bear country to me."

"Oh, they're out there all right," I said. "They like to raid corn fields at night."

"Yeah? I want to get a postcard of a bear. Maybe you'll tell me where I can obtain one?"

He was my age in his forties. His nose was the snub kind you see on little girls which was laughable in a face so manly. Wrinkles or scars slanted up from the corners of his eyes like wings or horns more burgundy colored than black. Like I said his jacket was tight on him and where the sleeves shrank back I could see the veins on his arms which throbbed outwards almost to the bursting point and would have been easy to poke an IV into. Don't ask me why but it was those veins that made me guess.

"You're army."

He beamed. "Twenty-three years!"

"You're a lieutenant. No, a sergeant."

"Master sergeant!"

"You're Sergeant Cobb."

He smiled even broader. "So he talks about me!"

Already the trap.

"He writes about you in his letters."

"A fine soldier! Makes us all proud!"

"You came all the way up here to tell me that?"

I thought it was smart to call his bluff right away but he ignored me and waved his arm toward the hills.

"He's always explicating how great it is up here, raving on about how pretty the beaches are and how the girls are so elegant and about the bars and restaurants and clubs. Makes it sound like paradise on earth so I always wanted to peruse it for myself. Yes, ma'am. His eyes would light up just telling me about it all. And now I can see why."

Beaches? Blondes? Nightclubs? He might as well have added on roulette wheels and roller coasters. And the funny thing is Cobb looked around like that's exactly what he saw.

"A fine soldier, always volunteering, always ready with a quip. Out on a route march we came to a river and I required someone to swim to the other side. You think any of those other effeminate no-account spoiled mamma boys would volunteer? Chop chop your boy's hand shoots right up. 'Master Sergeant Cobb,' he says like a real man. 'I know the river is full of evil cottonmouths and water snakes and crocodiles and leeches and my chances of getting unscathed to the other side are approximately zero but if it's for the good of the unit I'll gladly give it my all.'"

I looked him right in the eye. "Sounds like Andy all right."

"You know that song by King Cole they're always playing on the radio." He started singing. "Bring out those lazy hazy days of summer! I think old Nat must be thinking about life right here."

It's hard to describe his voice because it changed nearly every sentence but imagine a flat Midwestern accent combined with sounding like an Englishman in a war movie adding in a drawl like Amos and Andy or a Baptist preacher. Either he was trying to confuse people with it or he was pretty confused himself.

But right from the start I was storing up things about him I could use to fight back. He considered himself a ladies' man. He liked to talk a lot with big words thrown in. He enjoyed playing games. I knew when he left off bullshitting he'd be dangerous and the trick was to know when the bullshitting stopped.

"You must be tired after your bus ride, Sergeant Cobb. Luckily, I have some beers in the ice box."

He switched to Amos and Andy now even rolled his eyes. "Thank you kindly, ma'am!"

I sat him down on the porch while I went inside. I knew Andy was in his hiding place by now so what I mostly worried about was blurting out something that would give him away. The mosquitoes were bad so I lit a citronella candle and brought it back out with me even though it wasn't yet dark. Cobb wrinkled his nose at the smell and I thought well here's one more bug I have to get rid of but all he did was sit back on the rocker and put his feet up on the rail.

"Bottle okay?" I handed him two.

"You dwell alone here?" he asked tilting one back. "No husband around?"

"No husband around."

"No gentleman friend? Must get lonesome at night. Big place for a lady on her own. Does it get lonesome?"

"Nothing I can't handle."

He smiled like I was doing better now and he was really enjoying our little duel.

"So, how is Andy?" I said.

"Andy?" He looked puzzled like the name was new to him.

"It's been a long time since I had any letters. I understand you're shipping out."

He wiped the suds off his lip. "Fine soldier, makes us all proud."

"You're not going to Vietnam with them?" I handed him another beer.

"That's a lachrymose story. Been there twice. Two tours and the second was even better than the first. Got this minor wound in my shoulder here, those VC insurgents shot straight for a change, so they deployed me over to Louisiana to instruct all the youngsters and it breaks my heart not to go over with them and show them the sights."

I handed him his fourth beer. The longer he talked the louder his voice grew so it seemed like he knew Andy was hiding in the house somewhere and wanted to make sure he heard every word. It was all about Vietnam and how much fun it was. The weather was perfect the accommodations were luxurious anytime you were at all concerned about anything all you had to do was pick up the phone and call in an air strike and go back to bed. The officers were handpicked for their leadership abilities all they cared about was the welfare of their men and the local people really appreciated them couldn't do enough to make them feel at home.

I handed him his fifth beer.

And as much fun as it was out in the field that was nothing compared to how enjoyable the leaves were and when you saw how enjoyable the leaves were you wondered why you had wasted so much time back in the States. There were bars in Saigon three blocks long and behind every stool stood a gook waiting to take your order or fix you up with some weed or find you a girl all you had to do was ask and ten seconds later it was yours. Not just any booze either but the finest whiskey in the world and not just any weed but the purest money could buy and not just any girl but

Eurasian ones meaning their father was a Frenchman and their mother was a gook and there was no better way to mix races at least not when it came to a bar girl's looks.

I handed him his sixth beer.

Sure they were a little small on the boob side but that was more than compensated for by their asses which were tight enough to strike a match on and just a little bit bigger than a man's palm. You could control them like a puppet just by putting your hand on a cheek and they would smile for you and make a fuss over you and if you kept squeezing you could generate just about any expression you were in the mood for and if their smiling got boring you could always squeeze a little harder and make them wince. After that it could be anything and that included having two girls suck you off at the same time which was the sweetest thing a man could hope for in life it was worth going over there just to experience.

"All that I'm describing is for a black man," he said real amazement on his face. "You double the pleasure if your boy is white."

I'd had that done to me before where a man starts being crude and waits for you to slap him down and keeps getting cruder if you don't. But the longer he went on that way the safer I felt especially with him downing those beers. The sun sliced in on us through the porch rail but it didn't have the power it had earlier in the summer and all it did was turn his Budweisers copper.

I gave him another one wondered how he could drink so much and not have to pee. For all he rambled on about Vietnam it turned out what he really wanted to talk about was China.

"Shit ma'am, that's where the real peril lies. You think a piss ant country like Vietnam can cause us any peril?"

China was out to get us Vietnam was just a sideshow before the real battle commenced. He learned that back in Korea when he was just a rookie watching those hordes come streaming over the ridges and okay it was just a word people used hordes but it was one thing to throw the word around and another thing to actually be crouching in a frozen foxhole watching hordes come at you hordes upon hordes you could machine gun all you wanted and the hordes kept coming.

Next time they would beat us. They were waiting for Russia and America to blow each other up then they would move in with their garbage trucks and sweep up the debris. World dominion had been their goal all along he had made a detailed study the truth was plain as day. Had I ever read the writings of Dr. Sun Yat Sen? Hell, people always talked about Chairman Mao but he was nothing he was only following the strategy set out by Sun Yat Sen in 1913.

I handed him his eighth beer but instead of opening it he leaned forward in the rocker and looked me right in the eye.

"You ever read old Sunny Yat Sen? You should, you'd be surprised at how he had history all planned. You think we influence anything? You think the Soviets do? You think the Germans caused trouble or the Japs? It's all there in his books, how the Chinks plotted and schemed, and now those peanut pissers have us right where they want us, all it will take is a few more years. Mean bastards, too. Who would you want your sister to marry, your basic Hebe or your basic Chink? Personally, I'll take the Hebe every time."

He burped belched staggered to his feet. "Scuse me, missus," he said in his southern drawl voice. I thought I had him then just another drunken good old boy soldier. He stumbled around to the bushes and I could hear him against the house and when he came back all the beer was hosed out of him and he was sober again sucking his stomach in bracing his shoulders back jutting his chin out like he was on parade.

"And now Andy's mom, I'll take that little tour you promised."

He held the door open pointed for me to go in first. I think he must have been bored with our game because he didn't bother trying to bullshit me anymore but walked through each room looking things over touching the walls picking up lamps and ashtrays like he was searching for evidence or secret panels or fingerprints. I did okay downstairs but once we got to Andy's bedroom my heart beat so fast I was sure he could hear it. Andy's old Boy Scout badges lay on the dresser and he picked them up and twisted them to the light.

"Fine soldier. Very proud."

I held my breath while he searched the closet but like the state police he didn't look any deeper than the clothes rod. There was only my bedroom after that and I said to myself search it yourself if you want to I'll be downstairs but just as I turned away I felt his hand grab my arm not so hard it hurt but pretty close like he was telling me he knew where the border was for pain and if he wanted to he could take me across.

My bedroom was in the same sorry state it's always in but it seemed to amuse him the unmade bed my pajamas on the sheets my bra and panties. "Pink, I like that," he said making his voice go husky and for a moment I thought he was going to lick his lips.

I never saw a man switch moods so fast. "Thank you for the tour, ma'am," he said when we went downstairs. He shook my hand very formally. "And now I'll be parting, but I appreciate your hospitality very much."

"Do you need a ride somewhere?" It was dark out now and the moon swirled the porch with silver cream.

"Bus station would be fine."

He didn't say anything on the drive but sat with his face pressed against the window like he was still hoping to see bears.

"I don't think there's a bus until morning," I said when we got to town.

"I'll wait."

"I should tell you something, Sergeant. This can be a pretty rough town on Saturday nights. Farm boys drive around looking for trouble. I'm not sure what they would do seeing someone like you."

He looked over at me now. "You mean a nigger?"

He laughed with that really laughed so it was like his back teeth went rolling over the front ones pushed on by his tongue. Nigger. Tough town. Farm boys. Night. Nothing funnier! He opened the door came around to my side waited until I rolled down the window and he could say one last thing.

"A lonesome journey for a man like me, going back to Louisiana. A long and lonesome journey."

There it was the line I'd been expecting ever since he first stepped off the bus. "Buy yourself a magazine," I said.

He smiled straightened back up waved his arm around in a big circle. "I can perish happy, having seen it here now. Yes sirree ma'am, I can perish happy."

I'd been mostly scared until then but that changed to anger pretty fast. So Cobb was tough enough to relish fighting farm boys but not brave enough to get through the night without getting laid! That was so typical it was the way Perry had been and it always made me want to laugh and scream thinking of their egoism thinking of them thinking that three minutes inside you was enough to do away with loneliness like it was a fluid they could pump into somebody else. Okay your problem now woman. Wasn't that what they were saying when they came? Cobb or Perry I could have screamed at them both. Loneliness? You have the nerve the arrogance the balls to use that word? I can tell you what loneliness is and I don't need a stubby little cock to illustrate my point.

I found Andy in the kitchen puffing on a cigarette which wasn't something he did very often. A Red Sox cap was pulled low over his forehead and when I came in he tried hiding his face.

"What happened?"

He shrugged. "Got bonked."

His cheeks were scratched one eye looked black and blue and when I lifted the cap back I found a cut nearly deep enough for stitches. I fetched some bandages a bowl of water sat him down under the light went to work.

"You going to tell me more?"

He winced under the iodine.

"I heard you bring him upstairs into my bedroom and then the closet. All along I figured he'd be the one to come find me. Seemed better if he found me outside so I pulled back one of the ceiling panels, dropped down into the mudroom and ran out the back door."

"You were hiding in the yard?"

"Kept going all the way to the woods. Pretty dark in there, pretty scary. Scratched myself on some branches then I tripped against a rock and got bonked. Finally decided to just sit down. What I thought about was how Danny used to take me back there and we'd balance along that old stone wall seeing who could get farthest without falling off. He always found things I didn't know about like arrowheads and moose antlers and woodcock nests."

I had the gauze all the way around his forehead now but I added on another wrap just to make sure.

"We sat on a stump and Danny told me, not bragging or anything, that he was smart and ambitious enough to be anything he wanted. He'd been thinking about it, too. The best thing in the world to be was a Hollywood producer. That's why he watched so many Westerns, to learn how. Then he laughed at himself the way he always did. 'I'll probably work in a garage like Dad,' he said. 'But you know what? It's damn well got to be my own garage.'"

"Is that why you're not in the mood to shoot anybody? Because of what happened to Danny?"

I said that casually like it just occurred to me though I'd been wondering about that all along. He shrugged his Andy shrug seemed really considering the idea then slowly shook his head.

"Nah, it's just that I don't really feel like it."

"Sergeant Cobb says you're a good soldier."

He sucked his stomach in sat up straighter perfectly imitated his voice.

"A fine soldier. Makes us all proud."

"He's a complicated man."

"I'll say. He warned us if we ever messed up or crossed him he'd hound us all the way to our grave. We called him Hound after that or Hell Hound. He'll drink too much, then go into town and beat up civilians."

"Civilians?"

"Chinks."

He took a drag on the cigarette then did something that surprised me. He brought his hand up through the smoke and gently patted my arm.

"Listen Andy. Mary Belcher from work has a going away party tomorrow afternoon and I have to go or people will be suspicious. You know the drill now, what to do if anybody comes?"

"Sure. Tomorrow night's the next Uncle episode. Ilya's temporarily gone over to the Russians so Napoleon Solo is on his own."

We both slept late in the morning and after that we picked berries until our hands were blue but at four it was time for me to go. The party would have been sad anyway since I'd known Mary for twenty years and hated the fact she was moving but worrying about Andy made it torture. It was seven before I could make an excuse and leave and I think Mary was hurt that I left so soon.

The fog was so thick I couldn't drive home as fast as I wanted. The first thing I heard when I got out of the car was Nat King Cole singing Lazy Hazy Days of Summer and it made me mad that Andy could be so careless with the radio but then the words stopped and there was a burping sound and when they started up again they were in a lower key. I walked from the barn around to the front of the house. Sitting on the porch under the bug light making his fingers wiggle like he was playing piano was Sergeant Cobb.

"I thought about you last night," he said. "Your lips, your eyes, your fine evil ass. I hate skinny bitches, no meat on them. Full breasted, that's what enamours me. Sweet Jesus Fuck, you're full breasted."

What startled me was the fact he had his army uniform on. Where had he gotten it? Yesterday he hadn't even carried a bag. On his sleeve were his sergeant stripes and over his chest a row of medals hanging down like slack little penises spray painted in gold. The uniform made his waist seem even smaller than before so I thought of the term wasp-waisted and realized for the first time how repulsive a wasp can be.

"You had a long walk from town," I said trying to keep my voice even.

He pointed toward the grass. Parked there under the locust was an Army jeep with a white star painted on the hood and an aerial looped over in a hoop.

"Andy's not here," I said. "You've wasted your leave or assignment or mission or whatever it was brought you here."

He swung his arm around in his favorite gesture the one that seemed to take in all the world.

"I never lost one before which is really saying something the crap they send me. Greasers and retards and hoodlums and frat boys and mental defectives. They draft them and send them to me to whip into line and somehow don't ask me how I do it. I embark them on that plane for Saigon and the government gives me another medal and my pay goes up ten dollars a month. I never lost one. Never lost one, goddamn one. But even worse would be los-ing that ten dollars."

He pushed himself up from the rocker came over to where I stood on the furthest edge of the porch. Like he was hot or his col-lar had suddenly become too tight for him he unbuttoned the top of his tunic until I could see the olive colored t-shirt underneath.

"Know something? If I had someone to help with the lonely part I would leave tomorrow chop chop, no questions asked."

He brought his hand up and I thought he was going to grab my arm but it kept going higher turned into a fist tapped me lightly on the chin. A love tap was that what it was supposed to be? I backed away but now his other hand grabbed my arm and like yesterday he squeezed just hard enough to let me know it could be a whole lot harder if he chose. He pulled me toward him very slowly enjoying every second in no hurry at all and then sud-denly sensing the bargain had been struck sensing by who knows what sign that I had agreed to it initialed our contract given in he pulled much harder and brought his lips down and pushed his breath into my ear.

"You're a prevaricating little cunt, but I like that."

He took me in through the dark up to my bedroom. I heard a scraping noise and figured it was Andy crawling to his hiding spot but it didn't seem high enough it seemed coming from down-stairs. Cobb didn't hear it he was way past the hearing stage now. For all his swagger he stripped off his uniform fast enough like it burned like it was hateful like it was poison.

I wasn't ashamed of what I was doing and I know that must confuse you but I don't know how else to explain. We had our bargain and it was the same bargain whores struck every night in their miserable rented rooms or unhappy wives made in return for being kept or tortured women made to protect who was dearest to them or to escape whatever trap held them or simply to survive. Cobb was lost in passion but that was okay he could buck and moan all he wanted to it was balanced by what I felt which was a protective instinct ten times stronger and harder and tougher than anything he could feel himself and was backed up by all the strength I gained from thinking of all those women who over the centuries had made the same bargain.

That's what I thought about as Cobb hunched over me. As it turned out I only had to think about it for a minute and a half.

He rolled off me grunted flopped his arm over my thigh. He was snoring soon enough. I listened the way you listen to a clock ticking not particularly liking the sound but not particularly disliking it either it was just this harmless mechanical thing in the dark. But then much quicker than I expected the sound stopped and when the sound stopped I became very frightened.

He climbed into his uniform even faster than he'd taken it off. He saw me staring waved his hand in something that could have been seeyou later alligator or wham bam thank you ma'am or just as easily could have been drop dead. He didn't step into the hall right away but leaned his head out and peered. The loaded shotgun was under the bed and if I had to I could quickly slide it out. I knew if I thought of Danny I couldn't touch the trigger but thinking of Andy I knew I could.

I put my robe on and followed him downstairs. He walked from one room to the next sniffing like a bloodhound and didn't care that I was following right behind. He went into the dining room but it was quiet and still. He went into the front parlor and turned the lights on then turned them back off. He walked down the hall in the moonlight then suddenly swerved left into the TV room and went right over to the set. He stood staring down at it then squatted and put the back of his hand flat against the screen.

Just that little gesture putting the back of his hand against the screen like a doctor checking a patient's temperature and then with a little nod to himself he was gone.

I was a fool not to read that gesture better. So sure was I of things that I didn't even bother waking Andy up before going to work though I suppose not wanting to face him had something to do with it too. I had punched in at the hospital and gone to my locker when I saw Wendy Poor the meanest of our aides talking to three other aides by the coffee machine.

"What a commotion!" she was telling them. "It was by the town hall and I could hardly squeeze past there are so many state troopers. There are these other guys in suits and sunglasses and they look like they mean business."

"Drug raid," one of the aides said knowingly.

"Drugs baloney. It's a posse and leading them is this big nigger soldier driving a jeep."

I walked as fast as I could to the stairs and by the time I got to the parking lot I was running. My heart shook so hard it blurred any thoughts that formed so I couldn't come up with a plan all I could think about was getting to the house before they did. It was a ten-minute drive for me and twenty minutes for them which didn't give me much time. I drove faster than was safe but then all of a sudden I noticed a yellow rectangle in my mirror that was going even faster honking its horn to pass.

It was the truck from the Wooden Shoe that dilapidated psychedelic truck that usually could only huff and puff along but now went so fast it was like they had poured LSD straight down its tank. And not just its tank. On the flat bed of the truck holding on for dear life were four or five girls dressed like can-can dancers waving with their free hands and blowing kisses even though there was no one along the road to watch. Music blared from the radio this pounding rock and roll. That was on back. Up front in the cab things were different. Three men sat with their shoulders pressed tight as bookends and they looked as grim and determined as the girls did gay. The driver honked again and where the road straightened out they went speeding past me downhill.

A party I decided an outing of some sort a merry jaunt and my mind jumped around so frantically it wasn't capable of making any more sense of it than that. I decided if they could drive that fast then so could I so I shoved my foot down and went careening around the last curve before home. When I wrestled the wheel back I got my second big shock of the morning. The truck instead of racing past the house braked hard and turned in.

Andy stood outside on the grass looking startled and embarrassed and bashful and confused all at the same time. He had just his underwear on and when the girls sprang down from the truck and rushed over to him he covered up his groin with his hands.

The girls didn't care about that. One was August and the other was the Dahlia girl I remembered from the night Lilac's baby was born and another was Kit the Viking who had been so steady. They danced around him like he was a Maypole they were throwing flowers at and all Andy could do was stare at them in bewilderment because he just couldn't get his mind around what was happening.

Granite jumped down from the cab with two of his henchmen one of who looked like General Custer in a cavalry outfit with a mustache and ringlets. He had a bugle he blew now as loud and triumphantly as he could. Granite knocked it away from him with one brutal swipe then marched over to me not in the mood to waste words.

"Get him in the truck."

I was so surprised and frightened I must have froze because I could see his expression change to disappointment and contempt that I of all people could freeze. In the distance we could hear sirens now lots of sirens closing in fast.

He signaled one of his men to keep watch on the road then went over and pulled the girls off from Andy. "Get in the goddamn truck!" he yelled.

Andy still looked bewildered and instead of doing what Granite ordered he began backing up toward the house. He's going to bolt I decided going to turn and run to the hiding place and if he does that he's finished. The sirens really howled now we probably had no more than three or four minutes and it was only then when the pressure was greatest that my head finally cleared.

I grabbed Granite's arm which was like grabbing hold of a nail. "Ask him politely," I said.

Granite stared down at me. "What?"

"Ask him nice!"

He made a what the hell gesture went over to Andy put a brotherly arm around his shoulder and said something too low for me to hear. It must have been as polite a request as one man ever made to another because between one second and the next Andy without even a wave or last glance back was running over to the truck and the men were boosting him up on back and the girls were laughing and singing and waving their arms in excitement and delight. Granite climbed up to the cab and threw the gears into reverse and spun the truck around speeding off in the opposite direction from the sirens more on the shoulder than the concrete so stones flew up pebbles branches sticks like spray from a motorboat heading away from all the sirens all the confusion heading away to the hills away to the forest away to that brave foolish dream of a country where no one could find them or touch them or hurt them.

For just one second one terribly short second I felt like shouting in victory and triumph then a second later I felt sick from exhaustion and the little smear of loneliness left in my womb. I had four minutes before the posse arrived with their sirens and cruisers. I decided to wait for them inside the house and the room I ended up in was the TV room and what I ended up staring at was something I'd totally forgotten about after Andy came home which was that little peel of wallpaper I had discovered writing beneath then immediately pasted back up. And that's where they found me and for the whole time they shouted bullied threatened I became just an empty headed gal with nothing on her mind but walls and wallpaper and prettying up her home.

They tore apart so much of the house it's a wonder they didn't rip off the wallpaper and save me the bother. When they finally left instead of trying to clean up their mess I started scraping and discovered the writing wasn't just doodling but a woman's story. When I started reading all I was aware of was how different she was from me it was all so far back in time but soon I realized how similar we were to each other and how fifty years is nothing but a second a flick of the eyelashes a snap of the fingers a whisper.

I don't have to tell you this about Beth because it's how you must feel yourself. After I finished her story I worked in the sewing room until the walls were all bare. Seeing this running my hand along the smooth plaster I felt like a little girl who has a secret and will burst if she can't tell it to somebody. Like that except it's not an itchy spot in my tummy or a buzzing on my bottom or a tugging on my pigtails or however it feels to a girl. My heart will burst if I don't tell my story to somebody and that doesn't feel like a figure of speech but the simple truth and the feeling hurts even worse because there's not a single living person I can tell.

Nurses at work always tease me about my pens about how I carry so many colors and why bother since all we ever write are memos to doctors or the charts on beds. Now that I had a wall to write on I was happy to have so many and I spread them out across the floor like they were paint brushes I could pick up or put down according to my mood. In a way I can't explain the bare walls are DEMANDING I write on them so it isn't just the secret in me bursting to get out but something outside me yanking just as hard.

Stripping the paper off reading Beth's story has been good for me it's helped get me through these first days after my sweet lovely foolish boy left but the part of me that will never heal is the part I need to write down. Everybody has a secret they can't share but MUST share and it could be who you loved or who you hurt or lied to or cheated or envied or fucked or didn't fuck or a secret shame or crime or failure or even a secret triumph no one knows about but you and all that goes on the wall or stays inside you and rots.

I'm telling you this in the last few seconds before I finish my writing and cover it up with wallpaper that might not be stripped off for another fifty years. First Beth then me now you. We are the sharers of secrets we are sisters we are the women who write on walls.

Four

THE writing slanted like a ramp toward the floor but didn't quite touch. In the six-inch space left blank Dottie had inserted a photo, wedging its bottom edge into the molding that formed the border with the fractured maple of the floor. Vera reached down and gently tugged to see whether it would slide out without having to use her scraper, and when it did, brought it over to the kerosene lamp where she could study it closer.

It looked like an old-fashioned Polaroid, the kind that only took one minute to develop. Andy—it could only be Andy—stood on the back steps of the house with his arms outstretched, holding what appeared to be a pie fresh out of the oven, since he held it with a fuzzy white mitt. He was younger looking than she imagined and more handsome, with his blond hair in a crew cut that was long enough now it could have used combing. He wore khaki work pants and a white t-shirt, and it was this last that made the photo seem ancient. No logos in those days, no shaping, just that bleached, angel-like whiteness billowed out from his chest. His expression seemed a bit exasperated, as if his mom had badgered him into posing, but patient enough now that she was actually snapping it. The gentle shyness she had described was plain enough on his features—just the kind of boy Cassie had felt comfortable with back in high school. No brain, no jock, somewhat bashful, good with cars.

He wasn't the only one in the picture. His mother had posed him on the steps, with the kitchen window to the left; on the glass Vera could make out the reflection of a woman who must be Dottie, captured in the act of taking the photo, an accidental self-portrait. Between the dullness of the reflection and what the years had done to the print, there wasn't much visible, just a watery, lemon-colored shape distinct enough she could define it as feminine. There was a smeared half-circle that could have been her forehead and hair, a minute silver flash that could have been earrings—but at least she was looking at her, and it hit her even more powerfully than seeing Andy. Reading, she had pictured Dottie liking bright, extravagant colors. So yes—lemon made sense. It would have been her favorite summer dress.

There was no date stamped on the back, no identifying information. She brought it back to the wall, got down on her knees by the molding, made sure she tucked the edge back exactly the way she found it. Staring at it had given her an idea. She went out to the kitchen, turned on the ceiling light, propped open the door so its brightness could arc across the first twenty feet of backyard.

She had discovered the blueberry bushes on her very first walk around the house, but she hadn't checked to see whether they still held any berries. Seeing the picture, she had immediately decided that this is what she must do—go out to the bushes Dottie had planted, the ones Andy had helped her pick for their pie, find a berry, just one berry, and hold it in her hand.

She pushed past the screen of briars to where the bushes grew thickest, forced her way into their middle, grabbed a high branch, followed it back to its woody core, then ran her hand back out again, flattening the leaves. They felt good against her skin, the oval texture with a hint of wax, but she found no berries on the first bush, none on the second, none on any of them, though she searched very hard. Did blueberry bushes have a life span? If they did, then theirs had long since expired.

Disappointed, she followed the widest beams of kitchen light around to the front, suffering the same wild restlessness she had experienced when she finished reading Beth. As before, she thought about getting in the car, but that seemed too drastic a response—she wanted space, not separation. Never in her life had she gone so long without driving. Between Jeannie stocking the house like a bunker and her absorption with the walls, it had been weeks now and she wasn't even sure the car would start.

Other than walking back up to the deserted neighbor's, there was only one place left to explore. Ever since she had arrived and particularly now that she no longer trusted the radio, the sound track to her days had come from the little trout stream across the road. It had sounded strong and percussive those first few nights, to the point she thought she could discern pebbles and stones clattering against each other in the current, but now that it hadn't rained in so long it seemed more a soft neutral humming that suggested the play of molecules, not rocks.

It was mucky, the first few steps off the road, but then she came onto the hard gravel plain the stream had scoured through the swamp. The rocks were slippery with moss, she could easily break her ankle, and so she sat down on the first flat boulder she came to, pulled her sandals off, let her feet dangle in the water. Even on a moonless night the stream seemed to generate its own incandescence; finding her ankles, it covered them in frothy white. The current ran north toward Canada, and, like so many other things here, gave her the sense that the land was tipping away from America, going stubbornly off in its own direction.

She enjoyed that feeling. She enjoyed the cold velvet clutch of the water on her skin, the way the sensation was so intense and immediate and yet carried with it memories of wading barefoot when she was little on one of her family's rare summer picnics. It made for two currents, two layers, and she couldn't have said which was the more satisfying.

Did Cassie have memories like that? Not for the first time, she wondered about bringing her here once her sentence was over, to see whether quiet and solitude could help her take the first steps toward healing. There were complications, of course. How long it would take for her discharge to go through. Whether Jeannie and Tom would want to have the house for themselves. Whether, quite simply, she and Cassie could still find a way to talk to each other, repair all that had been torn. If she did come, then the first stop would have to be the stream. Cleansing, baptism, purification. Vera never believed in any of those notions, they were just empty words and Cassie would frown if she used them, yet it was exactly this that she needed. After a month in the stockade of Fort Sill, Oklahoma, to be plunged into an icy trout stream and, shivering from the shock of it, begin the long slow process of absolution.

For herself, she was beginning to understand how a person could fall in love with this forgotten corner of land, or, like Dottie, fight through to a grudging, tough-love kind of acceptance. Like a lot of hard places it was more beautiful at night. She had been here long enough that the stars had changed slightly their pattern, so Vega stood directly overhead now and the long stretch of Andromeda rose in the east. A pleasantly astringent smell, part marigold, part sage, wafted downward from the cloud of the Milky Way. Could stars cast off smells? If it was possible anywhere it would be here.

Tom claimed there were trout in the stream, though they must have been tiny ones, the water was so shallow. What would they make of her, if they watched through the foam? She stayed on her rock until the shivering spread upward from her toes; she had to rub them to get the circulation back to the point she could walk. The flinty gurgle of the stream drowned out the crickets, but back near the house their chirping took over, and much later, when she finally left off her fixed staring and let herself collapse back on the mattress, the strong tropical clatter of the sound cushioned her over into sleep.

Dottie wrote about the determination to protect her son that had come to her in the night. Beth's decision to buy the book of poems had come to her suddenly on a winter's morning. And now it was her turn—she woke up before dawn feeling an energy and purpose stronger than she had known in months. If anything, its suddenness made her suspicious, so for most of the morning she half-expected the determination to disappear. But it was the suddenness that disappeared. She realized that, without it ever becoming explicit, her purpose had formed the very first moment she had uncovered Beth's writing and learned, in that instant, that walls would accept ink as readily as paper.

The dining room was the last room needing to be stripped. Since that first tour of inspection on the day she arrived she hadn't stepped into it even once; now, dragging in the ladder and supplies, she realized it was by far the most attractive room in the house. This was largely due to the three tall windows with their transoms of stained glass—facing north, they still let in more light than the other rooms enjoyed, so it was the only place in the house that wasn't shrouded in dust. Even the wallpaper, Dottie's wedding cake pattern, the pink-veined white velvet, didn't look quite as awful as it did in the hall. The flooring was in better shape, too—shiny enough to slide on if she wore slippers. There was a positive, accepting aura to this space, she didn't know how else to put it, and it seemed to exist independently of anything in the room itself.

She started scraping by the door. The first strip was hardest because she half-expected to discover more words beneath the paper and it made her wary. Finding none, it became easier, though it still involved the same slow, painstaking work as before. Using the scraper like a knife to get the edge started, sliding it under the largest piece possible, prying, lifting, pulling— and then the whole process repeated again, clearing two or three inches at a time. One long strip shaped like a map of Chile she worked on for three hours. The air was drier in the room, it seemed to have petrified the paper, and she was carving out deep fjords and winding bays and whole estuaries before Chile came off.

Working this hard, it was impossible to remember ever having worked on another task, to the point that teaching, housekeeping, waitressing in college all became memories from a distant life. When she took a break she looked down at her hands and they had become a scraper's all right, there was no other way to describe them. Palms red and scratchy, veins cord-like on her wrists, the pads on her fingers puckered and cracked. No amount of massaging or stretching could soothe the tightness in her forearms—every tense molecule in her body seemed to have migrated there to hold a convention, party, whoop it up. And yet the odd thing was, when she looked down to examine it, the flesh on her arms, even after all that hard work and tenseness, seemed to have become noticeably looser in her time there, grainy the way wet sand is, slack, so it looked like it would look when she turned sixty.

She understood now that without Beth's and Dottie's stories leading her on she would never have had the stamina to do this. Even now, with only one room left to strip, she wouldn't have been able to finish without this sudden surge of confidence and energy that had come to her in the night. Stripping the other rooms, she had been content just to get the top layers off and ignore the little flecks of paper underneath, but now she needed to clear these off too until the walls were perfect.

Or almost perfect. As bare as she made them, they still weren't quite ready. Mixed in with the supplies was a package of sandpaper, and she used the finest to scrub away at the rough spots on the plaster, the grainy upsurges, the rice-sized bumps, until her finger could trace a line from the window to the door around to the windows again without hitting anything that wasn't smooth. It was fussy of her, compulsive, anal—but she trusted the feeling, it was part of her confidence, this overwhelming sense of being ready at last.

It took her two full days to scrape the paper off, then another day to do the sanding, so it wasn't until the morning of the fourth day that she started writing. With all the supplies Jeannie had left her there was one essential she had missed—pens—and it was only because she found a ballpoint to go along with the roller point in her purse that she didn't need to drive to town. She had the worst handwriting of any middle school teacher in the country, so she decided to print, to take pains over it, make the words perfectly legible. She wouldn't start so high that a ladder would be needed and she wouldn't go so low anyone would ever have to kneel to read, and yet, with four big walls to work on, she should have more than enough room.

She started with the roller pen from her purse, but the plaster sucked the ink in too greedily, so she immediately switched to the ballpoint which worked much better, though she often had to bring it down from the wall and shake the tip. And yet the walls still seemed greedy—no matter how fast she wrote, they constantly demanded more. Always before, writing on paper, she felt the space between words as little obstacles or hurdles, ones she could only jump by writing the most obvious banalities or cliches; now, the needed words seemed sensitive to her pauses and leapt in quickly on their own.

It was hard pressing horizontally, not down—like using a blackboard, though all she ever wrote there were lessons where the chalk skated across the surface on its own. With the walls, she had to position her body just so, slide her fingers down the barrel of the pen from where they went normally, and the difficulty of this made her feel even closer to Beth and Dottie. My fellow contortionists! Their arms had trembled the same way hers did; their shoulders had known the same nagging pain. It was hard, she constantly had to stoop, reach, swivel and twist as she moved along the wall, and yet that other tightness, the bone-deep soreness, the weakness, the weariness of soul, all disappeared the moment she began writing.

I played a game with Cassie when she was little. On Friday nights, as a special treat, we always went out for dinner somewhere simple, a family restaurant where they had a salad bar and brownie sundaes. Dan would meet us there late because of having to square away whatever construction job he was working on before the weekend. Cassie crayoned horses and dogs on her placemat while we waited, and that was fun for a while, but if it got really late and she had already finished her quota of rolls and crackers, I was forced to improvise.

"Watch the people coming in," I told her. "I bet you the cherry off your sundae that every one of them touches their face when they come through the door."

Her eyes danced upwards in amazement. The "Cassie dance" we called that, we saw it so often.

"Every single one of them?"

I nodded. "When they get in as far as the cash register and see everyone looking up. Yep, you watch. They touch their nose or ears or glasses and sometimes their chin."

And of course I won. This was a great revelation to Cassie, that adults could be so nervous in a fussy, impossible-to-control way. Every Friday after that she would stare over her menu at the people coming in, checking out everybody's little tic, with a wise, knowing expression on her face a lot older than her years.

That's what I was thinking about when they led her into the courtroom in June, our harmless little game. And what's more, I knew she was remembering this, too, knowing I was sitting there watching. She must have been nervous, the temptation to touch her hair or nose must have been irresistible, but she wasn't going to give into it, that simple human weakness. She paraded in, wearing her dress uniform with the flesh-toned stockings, the tight-waisted skirt—paraded in, marching at attention, and just when I thought she was going to at least nod to us or thinly smile she stopped and snapped off a salute toward the flag. Beside it, standing three abreast behind a high metal table, the members of the court martial saluted crisply back.

Not my girl, I remember thinking. It's impossible to describe how savagely the thought came, and how, for the space of twenty seconds, it afforded me relief. But of course it was my girl, the uniform couldn't hide that, nor the rigidly obedient way she stood.

Two of the judges were majors, one was a sergeant—all three were female. The MP who followed Cassie in was female, the prosecutor was female, so for a moment it resembled an elaborate sorority initiation during which Cassie had been ordered not to smile. The lieutenant they had assigned to explain things to us was a woman, too, and the defense counsel, Captain Sosa, was the only male in the room besides Dan.

It was a small room, with only three rows of seats. The one spectator was a young, nicely dressed woman who I immediately recognized, though without quite remembering her name. She wasn't a reporter—she held no laptop or pad—but I had seen her face on television and if I hadn't been so focused on Cassie I would have come up with her name a lot sooner than I did.

What else? Pear trees out the window, the leaves looking dry and shriveled, though it was only June. The air-conditioning blowing too strong, so even the majors shivered. A tornado warning on the wall telling us where to run if sirens went off. Dan reaching to find my hand, me tugging it back from him. The cricket chirp of the stenographer's machine. A sign over the judges' table, Fort Sill Oklahoma, in flowing cowboy script.

The whole atmosphere stayed calm, as if the tornado had come and gone and we the survivors must quietly go about our business. Like that—and like it had all been rigidly choreographed, and everyone, even Dan and me, were playing our assigned parts.

The reporters, cameramen, bloggers and journalists had already left town. Cassie wasn't pretty enough, her crime wasn't sufficiently brutal, to capture their interest. It had been the first series of trials, the general court martials held a week ago, that had created all the excitement—Cassie was small potatoes in comparison. She had not tied any of her prisoners to a leash or covered their heads in panties or pissed on the Koran or sodomized them with a broomstick or forced them to adopt "stress positions" while country music blared through peanut-butter covered pods taped to their ears. She had not been stationed at Abu Ghraib prison nor played a role in the crimes committed there. As a guard with the 363rd Military Police company of the 500th MP Brigade, U.S. Army Reserve, she had been assigned to watch the overflow prisoners who had been sent to a detention center near the city of Al-Kut——Camp Patterson, called by the MPs "Camp Patty."

While on duty there, guarding what few female prisoners Patty held, she had gotten a call on her cell phone from a sergeant telling her to hurry down to Tier One Alpha. This same sergeant had asked her to play pool the night before and she had said no. Now, afraid she had hurt his feelings, she said she would be right down.

When she got there, he and his fellow sergeants led her to a shower stall at the end of the cell block. A dead Iraqi lay there in a pool of crusted blood. All night he had been subjected to an interrogation that involved not only beatings but a handler holding back a barking, snarling German shepherd inches from his face. He snapped under this. When the interrogators finally left to get breakfast, he began pounding his head against the cement wall of the shower stall and continued doing so until he was dead.

After wrapping him in ice, the sergeants called their friends among the other guards asking if they wanted to pose next to him for a souvenir photo before they carted him off on a waiting gurney. Cassie had been one of three soldiers who posed.

At the judges' table one of the shivering majors finally had enough—he waved the MP over to adjust the air-conditioning, which she did but only by standing on a chair. In the interval, the lieutenant assigned to explain things to us, Lieutenant Vidic, leaned over our laps and rapidly whispered.

"They'll be asking for her plea. It's not dereliction of duty since it wasn't her prisoner and the incident wasn't even on her tier. That's why it's only a special court martial, not a general. It comes down to whether or not under the Uniform Code of Military Justice she engaged in conduct bringing discredit to the military."

"Thank you, Lieutenant," Dan said, reaching across me to shake her hand. That was the fourth time he had done that since we arrived at the courtroom, shake her hand. Dan is stolid, he can do stolid so well, but right then at that moment what I needed was an agonized husband, a trembling husband, a husband on the verge of breaking down at what had happened to his girl.

"Guilty," Cassie said, the moment the air-conditioning quieted.

She looked tiny as ever, standing by the much taller MP. Doll-sized, barely one hundred pounds, with the bangs she had worn since she was seven exaggerating the effect even more. She was always forgetting to put her contacts in, and the only expression on her face was the vaguest of squints. Other than that? I could see her acne was better. She looked like she had been eating okay. I didn't like the rigid way she stood at attention.

Between us and the front sat the woman I mentioned, so I had to look past her shoulder in order to see Cassie. She was not much more than twenty-five or twenty-six, dressed in an attractive brown suit that made her look like a businesswoman, crisp and very competent, though her frizzy red hair suggested something wilder. She sat formally, with her hands on her lap the way people do at funerals. Some stirring of the pear trees outside caught the light and she looked sideways toward the window. It was the kind of open face you immediately like, and the openness came mostly from her wide and caring eyes. Again, I wondered where I had seen her, and why, with no one else looking on, she had brought that look of sympathy to Cassie's trial.

As well as being choreographed down to the slightest detail, the trial moved very fast. The prosecuting officer and the defense counsel approached the judges with papers they dealt across the table like cards.

Lieutenant Vidic cupped her hand over her mouth and whispered:

"The prosecution goes first, now that they're proceeding to the sentencing phase. She'll be presenting matters of aggravation, things that tend to worsen the offense."

It was a photo she had placed in front of each judge, and I didn't have to be handed one to know what it showed. A young Iraqi man, detainee #143488 according to a sign balanced across his chest, wrapped in ice bags with bright red and green Arabic lettering. The ice bags packed right up to his chin, pressing it backwards like an icy bib, making it look like he was staring up at something stuck on the ceiling well behind him. Unshaven, his beard the same brown color as his skin, his nose and cheeks caked in blood, his mouth rigidly open. Eyes covered in duct tape. A body bag wrinkled beneath him like a sheet he had kicked aside. Black pointy hood like a sorcerer's flopping sideways toward his ear. Behind him, closer to the cement wall, a white plastic lawn chair, the kind you can buy at any mall. A fuzzy football-shaped something underneath its legs .

Squatting by his head, leaning over to make sure she posed in the same frame, Cassie. Brown t-shirt tucked into baggy camouflage pants, sand-colored with scattered chocolate-chip dabs. Green plastic glove. Big smile on her face, beautiful smile, the smile of someone who had never looked so beautiful, vivacious and incandescent before. The best photo of her ever taken.

The prosecutor, now that all three judges were staring down at it, felt confident enough to step back from the table.

"Please notice the defendant is not just passively posing, but makes a thumb's-up gesture to the camera while Sergeant Mendoza takes the picture with—" She glanced down at her pad. "Sony Cyber Shot Three camera. The prosecution contends that this gratuitous and vindictive gesture brings even more discredit upon the military than alleged in the original charge."

The defense counsel, who until now had seemed content to let the women run the show, cleared his throat.

"This can not be considered an aggravating factor, since it was merely the defendant's habitual nervous gesture. Specialist Savino is often very shy and never knows what to do with her hands in a photo, and this is where the thumb's-up gesture originates from."

Dan leaned over to our lieutenant. "That's true," he whispered. He straightened back up, whispered now to me. "You know that's true."

The major in the center pointed the prosecutor back to her seat. "Matters of mitigation?" she said, waving the defense counsel up in her place.

"Thank you, Major Adams. The guard dog involved in the incident became very agitated in the course of the night, to the point he was impossible to soothe, even by his handler. It was the defendant, Specialist Savino, who calmed him down and returned him to the kennel, thereby removing a potential threat from the tier. She stayed with the dogs all morning, talking to them and stroking them to make sure they remained passive. Every officer in camp marveled at her influence with dogs."

The sergeant judge now spoke for the first time.

"This is mitigation?"

"We believe that it is."

The major stood up. "Ten minutes before sentencing."

There was no reason to leave our seats. The judges disappeared out a side door which no one bothered closing. Cassie stood at ease, but still didn't look at us. Dan got up to flex his bad back. The clock on the wall ticked. The woman in front of us sat staring down at her hands, then turned suddenly around, like she was going to say something. Too late. Cassie, the prosecutor, the defense counsel, the stenographer and MP guard. They all stood to attention as the judges filed back in.

The sergeant had been chosen to read out the sentence. It was her big moment and she milked it for all it was worth—her voice wouldn't have been so deep and stern if Cassie had committed genocide.

"Under the Uniform Code of Military Justice, Specialist Cassie Savino, for conduct bringing discredit to the military, is sentenced to thirty days in the stockade, reduction in rank to private, and the forfeiture of half a month's pay."

Cassie saluted, turned ninety degrees and saluted her defense counsel, swiveled and saluted the prosecutor, then followed the MP out the door.

"That's that," Dan said, slapping his hands together.

Out in the lobby our lieutenant stood explaining what would happen next—Cassie's sentence would be served right here in Fort Sill, she said—when the MP came over and pulled her aside.

"Let's go," I said, but Dan wouldn't budge.

"Thirty days seems fair," he said. "Those Abu Ghraib guards got much more."

"Thirty days for smiling?"

"Someone told her to smile. You pose for a picture, the one who's taking it says 'Smile!' Anyway, it doesn't have anything to do with smiling, you know that as well as I do."

Dan closed his eyes, made a half-pucker with his lips, as if he were trying to squeeze something from his mouth that didn't come naturally.

"It's thirty days for defending her country. Thirty days for standing up for what's right. You think those detainees are Boy Scouts? They're killing our boys and it's a lucky thing they didn't kill her. She's over there on a mission and the mission sometimes involves things you and I can't stomach, but so what? You remember 9/11, how we didn't take our eyes off the TV for a solid week. That's two thousand reasons right there. If some raghead terrorist takes it into his head to kill himself I don't see why anyone over here should care."

I remember 9/11 I felt like saying. I remember how before that you were so funny and skeptical when it came to politics or world events, how you would always be on the side of the underdog, the army and generals and president could all fuck themselves as far as you were concerned—and how, that September night when we finally tore ourselves away from the television and went up to bed, you stopped by the window, looked out across the lawn and said "God bless America," not ironically, not as a joke, but with all the sincerity and passion your soul was capable of.

"Mrs. Savino?"

Our lieutenant was back. She came over and hesitated—it was obvious she wanted to talk to me alone.

"Cassie would like you to come see her tomorrow morning before you leave for home. She's allowed half an hour, but I think we can extend this some. It would have to be early. Is eight okay? The stockade abuts the south gate."

Dan nodded. "We'll be there."

"Cassie asked for her mother to come alone."

That's why the lieutenant looked so agonized, but her distress was nothing compared to the look that came across Dan's face. Crushed is too mild a word—his face jerked sideways like he'd been slapped.

"No problem," he said, smiling, and I know what that cost him. "We want to thank you again for all your help, Lieutenant. If you rotate back there, give them hell."

When we were alone again he took my arm.

"Let's go back to the hotel."

"I'd like to walk."

"In this heat? We have the car."

"I'll meet you there."

His face reddened. A little thing, but coming after the tension of the trial, his disappointment, it was exactly what could set him off.

"Okay," he said softly.

"It must be a woman thing," I said. Stupid of me, but I couldn't think of how else to lessen his hurt.

"That's fine. The two of you can have a good talk. Did you notice she didn't turn around and look at us, not once?"

I told him to be careful with the traffic and he told me to be careful walking in that sun. A marble staircase led down to the first floor, just like in a real courthouse. Once through the revolving door he turned left toward the parking lot, and I was still standing there trying to get my bearings when someone stepped out from the shadows along the wall.

"Mrs. Savino? My name is Pam Cord."

"I know who you are," I said.

In the courtroom, I'd gotten the impression of someone tall, which must have been from the formal way she sat, because I saw now she was shorter than me, maybe even shorter than Cassie. The sun brought the red out in her hair, and, seeing me stare, she patted it like someone putting out a fire.

"I saw you on TV last week outside the other court martials," I said, which was true enough. "It seemed strange to think you were at Cassie's, and I didn't really recognize you, not until the very end."

"Then you saw our demonstrations. The way the networks edited it made it seem like there were only a dozen of us, where there were hundreds. We still have lots of tricks left to learn." She tilted her head to the side and smiled. "Feel like coffee?"

She was parked in a handicapped spot—a small rental car yellow with dust. On our way out we had to pass the gatehouse and the sentry there snapped to attention and saluted. Pam gave him the finger, though with the windows being tinted, I don't think he saw. She drove fast, even recklessly—stop signs didn't seem to interest her.

"I'm sorry about your husband," I said. I thought that was important, to say that right away.

"Thanks."

She gave a lot of thought to where we should have coffee. There was a diner and then a drugstore with a lunch counter but she drove on past and turned left into a seedier part of town. The bars were here, the beer joints for soldiers, and she parked in front of the one that looked roughest.

It was early afternoon, there was hardly anyone inside, and, as in the courtroom, they were mostly female. The bartender. The soldiers playing pool. They were all dressed in desert camouflage, and when we walked through the door they looked us over with suspicion and hostility, which didn't seem to bother Pam Cord at all.

"Back here in the dark okay?" she asked.

The bartender took her time coming over. I ordered coffee. Pam ordered a beer, then waved toward the bar and changed that to vodka.

On television she always looked angry, so I wasn't prepared for how young she was, how friendly. She had become famous very fast, but I could tell that meant nothing to her. She had a trick of pointing off to where her words had gone, and she did this now, gesturing out the window toward what she had told me before.

"The media are already tired of us. Tired of me. I'm surprised they even gave us thirty seconds. Everyone went home afterwards, but I thought I'd stay on for your daughter's trial. I knew it was impossible, seeing her picture, that she could hurt anyone. At the first court martials all you had to do was look at their mouths to know they were capable of anything. Weak mouths, too gullible and frightened. The upper lip especially. If you want to search for cruelty, that's where you should look."

"Did you study my Cassie's lips?"

She shot me a look.

"Strong. Even. It wasn't her fault."

The bartender came over with my coffee and her vodka, stood with her hands on her hips until Pam paid. More women swaggered in now, sergeants, and over by the pool table things were getting pretty loud.

"You're wondering how the notorious Pam Cord got into the courtroom. We have friends—you'd be surprised. Lots of military think this is all wrong. Did you see that arrogant major staring down at me? She knew who I was. It made her nervous and that made me glad."

I noticed something about her when she took the first swallow from her drink—as professional and competent as she looked, she seemed tired, tense, even weary, and the only reason I noticed is because the vodka forced some of that away. Her hands never strayed very far from the glass. They were beautifully long and tapered, a model's, and yet red and chapped, like she still believed in washing dishes by hand.

"The only surprise is that even more of them weren't caught up in this. So I wouldn't be too hard on Cassie. They were badly trained—hardly trained at all. Reservists, amateurs. It all seemed just too weird to them, like a video game that moved too fast so they needed to smash the screen. The MPs who were prison guards back in civilian life ran things on the worst tiers. The hard site they call it. You notice how comfortably they use those terms?

High value detainees. Stress positions. Previously existing lesions. They can really talk the talk."

"Yes, it's awful," I said, to the coffee mug more than to her.

"They were pumped so full of anthrax vaccine it made them half-crazy. There was no privacy, hardly even toilets. Bladder infections, UTI's. There was hardly a girl who didn't have one. She had one, right?"

I nodded.

"There must have been pressure from higher-ups. You think privates like your daughter knew anything about Muslim customs, how to humiliate them? They were being told to soften them up for interrogation and they were being told exactly how. All the rest is just covering up."

You could see that her anger lay very close to the surface. Again and again she would try to lay out a simple, matter-of-fact explanation, find her voice rising, grimace, close her eyes, then start over.

"I had an e-mail from Jimmy just before he stepped on the mine. He realized it was all wrong by then, he wasn't stupid. We knew when he joined the reserves there was always a chance he would have to go fight somewhere. But we needed the money, the benefits. I hadn't found a job yet, and when I did it was only half-time."

I had a sudden intuition.

"Do you teach?"

She nodded. "Fifth grade art."

I smiled. "Middle school science."

"Middle school's hard, good for you ... So, we went into it with our eyes wide open, or at least that's what we told each other.

But we were blind of course. What bothered him most was how much the people hated us, and how he could put nothing against that except being nice to the Iraqi kids. He loved his men. He had the best men possible he wrote in his last letter. Everyone thinks I'm protesting the war just because of him, but it's because of his men and those kids and girls like Cassie and moms like you . . . It hurts to think Jimmy knew the bigshots were lying, but it would hurt even worse if he had believed them."

She told me about her organization, how it had started, how many parents, wives and husbands they had recruited and how more military families were joining every day. Who could speak out better than people who had loved ones over there, how could their voices not be heard? They couldn't be dismissed as radicals, they had given too much to their country. Their pain and despair needed an outlet, and she was no longer surprised at the depth of that anger and their determination to fight back.

Somewhere during this I realized she was asking me to join. It bothered me a little, it made it seem that all along she'd had this secret agenda to recruit me and Dan.

"I don't know how you get up the nerve to speak in public. It's all I can do to talk to my class."

It was the best I could come up with. I said nothing about the shame involved, that my daughter could smile so vivaciously over a dead man. Or the guilt, that I hadn't protected her from monsters.

"I would have said the same thing once," she said. "When I got invited to the White House after Jimmy died, I hesitated for a long time. I was still in the fog that descends, I couldn't see straight. Half of me wanted to buy into it all, the idea that he had died defending his country and fighting for freedom. The other half worried he had died for a lie. When the Pentagon called and said I was one of ten wives the president wanted to meet with to express his condolences I decided to go, because I thought maybe that would decide it, whether Jimmy was a hero or a sucker … Okay, here's where we get to the emotional part. Ready? More coffee?"

That was her way of ordering another vodka. When it came, she kept it in the middle of the table where the glass caught the light.

"It was a photo op for him, his poll numbers were sinking, so that's why the ten of us ended up in the Oval office with the generals and cabinet members and TV cameras. We stood in a semicircle on the carpet, the one with the presidential seal. I was toward the end and I could see him putting his arm around the other women's shoulders and saying something that judging by his little smirk was supposed to be a gentle joke. Despite the solemn men behind him he was enjoying himself greatly. There were three more women before me. I'm from Nebraska, it said that on the name tag along with Jimmy's name and rank, and I was absolutely certain he was going to say something about football, like 'Go Cornhuskers!' or something awful like that. He came up to me, a general leaned over his shoulder to tell him who I was, but his eyes fastened on my name tag and the word Omaha. 'Go Cornhuskers!' he said. Then he mumbled something that was meant to be comforting and moved on to the next woman in line."

She reached for the drink, put it to her lips, put it back down without tasting.

"They had refreshments for us in the next room. Punch and cake. There were knives on the table to cut the cake, surprisingly sharp ones. You know how you wonder if you ever had the chance to meet Hitler whether you would have the courage to kill him? Kill evil? That's what I was thinking about, staring at those knives. I thought of grabbing one and plunging it into his chest and then I thought about stabbing myself instead, and it didn't really matter, the important thing was to put death into that room as a fact, something real, not just the abstraction he and his henchmen could talk about so smoothly. I didn't have the courage, obviously. But all that emotion was still in me, and so when the president went before the cameras to make his little speech I screamed 'Butcher!' as loud as I could, and the rest you probably know about."

I knew about the rest. The uproar. The storm of attention. The hate. I read that she received more death threats in a day than anyone in the country, and I'm sure that was no exaggeration. Reading about her, seeing her on TV, I had been curious, I wanted to listen to what she said, but Dan always grabbed the remote from me and pressed mute.

Until now the only sound in the bar had been the click of pool balls, but the bartender turned the music on and three or four of the sergeants began dancing. I wondered what they would do if they knew the notorious Pam Cord was sitting there. Beat her? Shake her hand? I thought of what she said, how you could tell the brutal ones by the shape of their mouths, but with all of them chewing gum or sucking on beers it was difficult to tell.

I had the feeling, turning back to face her, that she was trying to decide whether or not to invest more emotion in me. As I said, there was a professional, even steely side to her, sympathetic as she was. And she was harried and overworked—I could see that, too.

"I haven't known you long, I can't read what's in your heart, but I sense you need to be part of something larger than just your worry over your daughter. Speaking personally, leaving aside matters of right and wrong, I've grown tremendously thanks to my involvement. I was big-time Barbie before that, all I cared about was shopping and clothes. So I've grown. Three cheers for me. But you know something? Despite all the uplift I've found and the solidarity and consolation, sometimes I wish I had grabbed that knife."

She finished her vodka, waved to the bartender for our check.

"Here's the business card they made for me, with my phone number and e-mail. Contact me directly, okay? My flight isn't until tomorrow afternoon. Are they letting you see Cassie?"

"Tomorrow morning."

"Tell her Pam Cord say it's not her fault. She's a victim, too."

She dropped me at the hotel where Dan waited. I didn't tell him about meeting her, mumbled something about getting lost. There was so much distance between us it was intolerable, so we lay in bed together watching TV, touching, holding each other, but not saying a word. It wasn't any easier in the morning. We packed so we could leave on time, paid the bill, ate breakfast in the coffee shop, talked about the fleecy clouds we could see out the blinds. I needed the car to get into the base, which left Dan with nothing much to do, but our waiter told us about a World War Two museum in town and that's where I dropped him off.

"Say hi for me," he said. "Tell her how proud we are."

The camp looked purposeful and empty at the same time. There was a tank, but it was an old one, harmless, mounted on a pedestal. I asked the first soldier I saw where the stockade was and she pointed to a low building I had already passed; it resembled the kind of motel you would only stay in if you were desperate.

Someone invisible buzzed me in. The visiting room had a high counter in the middle there was no way around. Strands of wire mesh ran along this counter like a ping-pong net, with metal stools on either side. There were no bars on the window, no surveillance cameras, none that I could see.

I sat there for a long time before Cassie came in. Alone, thank god—all the while we talked there was never any sign of a guard. She gave me a smile which didn't last very long. She touched one side of the ping-pong net and I touched the other. She looked pale compared to how she looked in the courtroom, tired. I had the feeling she would have been happier if she could have rested her head on the counter, not have to sit up straight.

"How are you?"

Any mother would ask that first. Any daughter would frown in just that way.

"Yucky. I've started. Of all the bad times."

"Are you taking anything? I have Motrin in my purse."

I started to dig.

"I don't think you better do that, Mom."

"For cramps."

"Uh, I'm a prisoner?"

"Well, do they have a medic? Ask them for some. Are you getting enough to eat?"

She shrugged. "Food was better over there. Tons better."

"Your hair looks nice. You're letting it grow long in back again. I've always liked it that way."

She patted it, frowned, but not as deeply as before.

"Dad sends his love."

"Yeah. Me, too. Tell him?"

"I will. Is there anything you need?"

"My phone back. They won't let me have it. It's going to be way boring."

"I could send you some books."

"I hate books."

"You never used to. You always begged us for ones about horses and dogs."

"Yeah?"

"Well, magazines then. Do you have any favorites?"

It was what I expected, a back and forth not much different than her phone calls from Iraq. Cassie's always had two looks, the shy quiet one she uses on most of the world, and the easier happier one she saves for us. If boredom is sometimes mixed in with this, if sometimes her eyes drift elsewhere, like all parents we had grown used to that a long time ago.

Like on our phone calls, I filled in her silences with the latest news.

"Dad's had to lay off three of his carpenters. It's really bad out there, all your friends you graduated with can't find work. I ran into Robbie Zimmer the other day and he's so sick of getting turned down everywhere he's thinking of joining the army."

"Robbie? He'd last three days."

"Nancy's moving to China, it was the only place she could find a job."

"China? Cool."

"Jeannie and Uncle Tom bought an old house way out in the boonies. They're going to fix it up and use it on weekends."

"Neat."

"Ida Rosenberg's taking my classes at school while I'm down here."

"Sorry about that."

"No, it's okay. That's not what I mean. School year's almost done anyway."

The army was clever with the ping-pong net, too clever, since it seemed more a barrier than solid bars would have been. Sitting there five minutes and already I wanted to rip it apart. Small talk was horrible, there was so much else to say, and yet, like with the net, it seemed impossible to find a way around.

Cassie was the one who tried first.

"So. Wheat did you think of my big trial?"

"We think you were picked on. Not picked on—singled out. Used for an example. Made a scapegoat. Blamed."

"Uh, that was me in the photo?"

"Of course it was you. But you were badly trained, you were shipped over there without any preparation. Higher ups must have known how bad conditions were."

"You haven't seen shit."

"I'm sorry?"

"That's what this terp kept telling me after the photos were taken. He and Truck."

"What's that mean, terp?"

"Interpreter. He and this contract interrogator, that's what they told me. Swear you have not seen shit."

"Truck?"

"Sergeant Mendoza. He's built like one."

"They told you to keep quiet?"

"Not exactly."

"Cassie?"

She shook her head, this time with real energy.

"It wasn't a cover-up, not at first. It was Truck's brilliant idea to snap the pictures, not only of the iced guy, but of everything they did before that, like the dogs and the pyramid and under-wear and what they did with sticks. He thought if he took pic-tures he could sell them for big bucks over the internet to rich guys who get off on that, seeing pictures of real-time interroga-tions. But then copies were made without his knowing and so he couldn't sell them anymore, they went on line for free, and that's when he got busted. All those guards on the hard site? He was their leader."

"Why didn't that come out at his court martial?"

"About doing it for money?"

She gave me the look every mother knows, the one saying how could I be so naïve, so totally clueless.

"But it's true, what happened? They called you to come down for a picture?"

"Yeah, it's true."

"And so you went?"

"I so went."

"And you smiled?"

"I so smiled." She cocked her head to the side, screwed her lips up, relaxed them into the bright, dazzling grin she had in the picture. "I can do it anytime I want."

That hit me hard, her doing that—speechless, isn't that what you're supposed to be? But if anything I had too many words, useless words, useless questions, and she only answered them with grunts. I saw her glance at the wall clock. We still had twenty minutes left, but already she seemed bored.

"I met an interesting woman yesterday," I said. Small talk—or maybe not. "She was in the courtroom, then we had coffee."

"I noticed. Some weirdo come to stare, I figured, but then she smiled over at me. Who is she?"

"Pam Cord."

The name meant nothing to her. She started complaining about her phone again, how she was going to go nuts without it—this seemed to be what worried her most. It surprised me, she'd never been particularly addicted before, and I was slow in understanding what emotion that masked.

The visiting room looked like a bad motel, and now, like at a bad motel, we could hear what sounded like a couple arguing three rooms down. Someone must have decided to turn the air-conditioning on, because it suddenly shot down on us like a fist, bringing with it the smell of french fries and ketchup.

"So," Cassie said. She dropped her eyes to her hands. "There's something else you probably should know about."

"About the photo?"

"After the photo. A week after. Something worse."

When she was little she had a funny grimace she made whenever she was nervous. Getting ready for a Christmas pageant, having to make a speech in class, even standing at the plate in softball. Her eyebrows, thin already, tightened into invisibility. Her mouth became tiny, her lips started trembling, she would suck in her cheeks. By high school she had outgrown that look—but here it was back.

"So, Cassie's shy, right?"

"You're better than you used to be."

She shook her head. "Cassie Savino is shy, right? She likes time alone. Great move, huh? Join the U.S. Army and get all the privacy you want."

I couldn't see where this was going.

"It must be hard on you," I said.

She shrugged the way people do when they're trying to shed words that don't count, grasp better ones just beneath.

"It was all so weird. Everywhere you looked and all the time, not just once and a while like at home. There were prisoners with no hands because they had been cut off for stealing before we got there, and no one thought that was unusual except me. No one thought the screaming was a big deal either. Little things got so they bothered you even more, until they became big things, way big."

"I'm not sure I understand."

"Lightbulbs, right? At home they're white, end of story. In the prison they were blue, these frosted Iraqi lightbulbs that hardly give off any light. The frosting was all cracked and peeling, so they looked like bad Easter eggs poked in the ceiling just above your bunk. I wanted to smash one, just to break apart the knot I felt inside all the time. After a while I realized smashing one wouldn't be enough, that I needed to smash at least a dozen to feel better. I dreamed about that, taking a baseball bat running down the hall smashing the ugly blue lights, and not just dozens either, but every last bulb in prison. That scared me, wanting to do that so badly. But that's not really what I need to explain."

The air-conditioning, as if listening, suddenly went still.

"So, I'm over there trying not to smash lightbulbs, and meanwhile every woman in the brigade is hooking up with someone. A boyfriend, a girlfriend. Doesn't matter which, but you better find someone to watch your ass, or else you're going to catch all kinds of shit from the tough ones. But I'm not doing it, Cassie's not playing along, and sure enough I start getting shit. A snot they called me. Barbie. Little Miss Virgin. I'm getting this morning, noon and night. It's like I either have to immediately hook up with someone or show them I can be as bad a dick as they are."

She looked up at me now—and, seeing her eyes, I wish she hadn't.

"There's a prisoner on the hard site named Rassoul or some weird Iraqi name. Truck had a friend called Nascar, he was so crazy about racing. Nascar was civilian but he was harder than any MI dude. He told us that Rassoul wasted three soldiers from 24th Brigade and raped one after she was already dead. They were trying to soften him up to get some high value intelligence but he was hanging pretty tough. They kept trying to scare him with all these stories about what would happen if he didn't play along. One of the stories was about the Ice Princess—about how the Ice Princess was going to come into his cell and make the things they had already done to him seem like kid stuff. She was going to cut off his balls for starters. The only problem was, it was only a story, the Ice Princess didn't really exist, it was just this crazy thing Nascar dreamed up."

Cassie reached her hand to the net between us, pressed it down with her fingers.

"I'd been volunteering in the kennel, the dogs had learned to trust me, and now Nascar's telling me I won't be allowed to anymore if I don't help them out by pretending to be the Ice Princess. They thought it would break him, having a girl come to his cell. That's all I was supposed to do, just duck my head in. It's eight at night, I'm just coming off shift, I go down there and they tell me to go into his cell and stare down at him like I was icy and mean. Yeah, roger that Staff Sergeant. No problem. I guess Rassoul believed their stories, because the moment I go in he cowers back in the corner and puts his hands in front of his balls. He had all kinds of gross cuts on his arms, they had interrogated him pretty good. I stared down at him for a few seconds then left, that's all it was at first."

"At first?" Never had my mouth been so dry.

"We kept a box of supplies at the end of the cell block. We called it the crap box because that's what was in it, random crap, including these green light sticks, the kind we played with as kids. Don't ask me what they were there for. Halloween parties or the Fourth of July or something . . . I go right over to the box and take out a light stick, go and find Nascar, have him take me back to Rassoul's cell. He holds him down from behind. I break the light stick in two and jab at it with my knife until I pierce the plastic skin. There's phosphorous in there, I knew that from fooling around with them as a kid. I cup the stick in my hands upside down so it won't leak. Nascar holds Rassoul's arm. It's like Jesus's arm—I remember thinking that with his beard and cuts he looked like he'd been pulled off a crucifix or something. I focused on the deepest cut and dribbled phosphorous down on it like a milky kind of soap. He screamed—right away he screamed. That surprised me because they told me he wasn't a screamer, no matter what they did to him."

Her eyes had never left mine, all the time she talked.

"It was over pretty fast. They pulled me out of the cell and I heard the door slam. I went up to my tier, changed my clothes, went to the kennel to play with the dogs."

Never left mine, not once all the while she talked.

"That's what I did, Mom."

She leaned closer to the net, but just when her forehead almost touched it she snapped herself back and sat at attention. Say something, her posture said. Ask me questions, shout at me, scream. But I only had one question that first second, one that hammered me. And then? And then? And then? Finish the suspense for me. And then I'm just kidding. And then I made it all up. And then I so had you, Mom, you actually thought I was telling the truth.

She must have seen that in my expression, my need for her to say she was just horribly kidding, but she only shook her head. We sat there in silence, waiting for life to get past this unbearable moment to whatever barely bearable moment came next.

That was the first second. The next one is harder to describe, since my thoughts came faster than I ever believed possible. I felt an overwhelming feeling of negligence, the kind that makes parents want to slap their foreheads again and again. All the things we had told her over the years, all the warnings and cautions we rained down on her—they broke over me in a wave, every last one of them in a detailed list. Don't forget to brush your teeth. Don't swim right after lunch. Don't jaywalk. Don't accept rides from strangers. Don't smoke. Don't do drugs. Don't drink and drive. Don't have sex before you're ready. All the standard don'ts, all that vigilance to keep her safe, and it was bullshit, it was crap, because while I spent nineteen years trying to think of every bad thing that could possible happen, I missed the real danger by a million miles. Don't torture anyone, I should have said, starting when she was seven. Whatever else you do in life, don't torture.

At the same time I tried sheltering under the same savage decision I briefly made during her court martial. Not my daughter. At the trial it had been my desperate attempt to renounce her, a trick that hadn't fooled my emotions for even a second. Now it came to me differently. Not my daughter—but it wasn't me saying that, it was the actual sense of life separating us, severing everything that held us close. And that feeling, of all the feelings I ever experienced, was by far the most terrible.

"It was just once," Cassie mumbled.

As painful as it was, that first breaking wave of emotion finished with me fast. I could feel it sweep on past my shoulders toward whatever blind, unsuspecting parents waited next on line.

"I felt numb afterwards," Cassie said. She pressed her knees together, twisted sideways on the stool. She didn't stare at me anymore—she already understood I could say nothing to put it right.

"You felt numb?"

She nodded. "Big time."

"How did your prisoner feel?"

Now she looked at me.

"Rassoul?"

"How did he feel?"

"I don't know. Frightened I guess."

"How old is he?"

"How old? I don't know. Twenty something. He had a beard. We called him Gilligan."

"Does he have a wife? Does he have kids? What town is he from?"

"I don't know. What difference does it make?"

"Does he have a mother? A father?"

"I don't—"

"For God's sake, Cassie!"

"Mom—"

"You tortured him!"

I yelled this loud as I could, as loud as I ever yelled anything. And that broke Cassie more than my words. Her face dissolved in tears—always before I thought that was just a cliché, but that's what happened, to the point where it made no sense as a face anymore, it was just this runny wet blob sloshing crazily from side to side.

"I can't hear you," I said, trying to make my voice gentle. She struggled to say something through the tears, but it took a long time before the words were strong enough to make sense. She was sorry at fucking up so bad, making us ashamed. She would leave the army and all that went with it, she was applying to veterinarian school, she had been saving this to tell me since she wanted to make us proud. She sobbed this out, and the sobs broke me just like my scream had broke her, and all I could do about it was reach my hand toward the net that separated us, the wire ping-pong net, and rest it there until she touched the other side.

"That's wonderful, Cassie," I said. "I'll tell Dad. No, that's wonderful news."

I kept my voice soft and eventually the sobbing stopped. A buzzer went off in the ceiling which meant our time was over. She stood up, smiled or at least tried. When she turned away to the door I saw fresh scratches on the back of her neck extending up past her uniform collar, the kind of bloody scratches that come when someone digs their fingernails as deep into their own flesh as they can possibly go, then rakes them savagely upwards.

Dad had taken a taxi to the entrance gate and waited for me there. As usual, he had made an instant buddy, the soldier on guard duty, and the two of them shook hands before he hurried over to the car.

"How was your museum?" I asked—simple words, but it was all I could do to get them out.

"Those were the days all right. Jitterbug music, K-rations, Rosie the Riveter. It's really well done."

"Do you mind driving?"

"Sure."

He didn't say much more than that, and even the obvious question was a long time coming.

"How's Cassie?"

"Fine. She misses her phone."

I said it too quickly—he noticed, but said nothing. Both of us needed coffee so we stopped at the first rest area we came to. While Dan waited on line, I found a quiet corner and made my call.

"Pam? This is Vera Savino. We had coffee together yesterday."

"Of course. How are you?"

"I know you're flying out later, and we are, too, but I wonder if we could get a few minutes to talk?"

"Flying out of Tulsa? We could meet at my gate. Let's see, I've got my boarding pass right here ... Gate twenty-seven at five-thirty. Would that work?"

"I'll see you there."

The drive took longer than we thought, there was the usual hassle checking in, and by the time we got through security it was already past four. "Be right back," I said, once we got to our gate. Dan glanced over his shoulder toward the rest rooms and nodded.

If Pam looked tired and harried yesterday, she looked even more so today, despite the crisp linen neatness of her skirt and blouse. She had her laptop open and was typing away while she talked on her phone, but she stopped the moment she caught sight of me through the crowd. We shook hands, but that wasn't enough for her, and she gave me a big hug.

"We don't have much time," she said, frowning.

At the counter was the sign saying where the flight was go-ing—Vancouver, which surprised me. Right above us was the TV monitor, but Pam gave it the finger and moved us to a quieter spot.

Before, when I wrote about my visit with Cassie, I left some-thing out. After she told me what she had done, after she cried, I asked her one question. Does anyone else know? She said no. Nascar of course and Sergeant Mendoza, but no one higher up than that. Good, I remember thinking. Good! She was safe, no one would find out about it, she wouldn't be charged with an extra crime. This is what I needed to explain to Pam, my shame at being glad, but how could I ever find the right way to begin?

She sensed my hesitation. "How was your visit with your daughter?"

"Difficult."

She nodded. "I know about difficult. Before Jimmy shipped out that last time, we talked about whether to try and have a baby. It wasn't about whether we wanted one, of course we wanted one, but whether or not the timing would work. It was all logistics, whether he would be home to help between deployments, whether or not his mom could come down from Chicago, whether I could get maternity leave. We even talked about whether it would be better to have a baby in the spring or fall, and we decided on spring, but the timing wasn't right for that, so—" She pressed her palms together. "No baby."

I took my deep breath. "Cassie and I had a game we played when she was little, something we did when we went out to eat. Watch the people coming in, I told her. Watch—"

That's as far as I got with my explanation. Pre-boarding was announced for her flight, and the line formed on our toes.

"You're flying to Canada?"

She nodded, ruefully nodded, and made a dismissive motion with her hand.

"The other members of the committee think I need a break. They might be right, too. What I've learned during our campaign is that most people can only be courageous in brief little flashes, that's all the vast majority of them can manage. One act of courage, one moment of heroic goodness, then poof—their capacity for doing it is gone forever, either that or they never get another chance."

"You've done lots of good."

"My little flash? Maybe. But they're right about my needing a vacation. What I worry about, really worry about, is how I'm going to be standing behind a microphone lecturing people who already agree with me that war is wrong, delivering my standard speech, and then I'm going to remember Jimmy and my anger gets the best of me and I blurt it out right in front of the cameras. 'I hate America! I hate America!' I'm going to yell that out and in one moment of weakness all the good work we've done comes crashing down in flames."

They were announcing her flight now, she began gathering up her things.

"Anyway, it's not a vacation, it's a reconnaissance. Apartment hunting. I'm thinking of moving there. I want to live in a country that doesn't bully. If I'm ever lucky enough to have a girl like yours that's where I want to bring her up."

"I'm going to call you," I said.

"My co-chair is a wonderful man named Hank Clarkson. He lost a son in Afghanistan. Here, I'll write down his number. We badly need new blood."

I took the card, nodded. "You better hurry."

"Love it or leave it, right? . . . You're a good listener. Cassie's lucky to have you."

I took the card out on my first day here, taped it to the refrigerator where I would see it every morning. Pam Cord had crossed out her name, written in Hank Clarkson's, the wonderful man, the man who lost his son in Afghanistan. But it's her I want to call. I want to volunteer when I finish here, though I need to ask how exactly I can help. Will I actually have the nerve? I think Pam is right, that most people find courage only in sudden flashes. Here at the end I'm remembering Beth's story, and how her husband Alan, so weak and manipulated, plunged into an icy river to try and save a man he hated. I can picture it so clearly, that brief moment standing on the bank before he made his decision. I will dive in, I picture him thinking. I will dive in. I will.

There's lots more work left of course. Jeannie's wallpaper, the rolls she picked out, waits in the parlor for me to hang. I must take my time with this, learn to use these new tools correctly. Brushes, yardsticks, trim knives, straight edges, seam rollers— tools not for ripping and tearing, but smoothing, pasting, pretty-. ing up. The paper is peach colored and gently Victorian, with a pattern that should be easy to match. Papering over won't take nearly as long as stripping off, and then the walls will be far too beautiful not to like. The paper will hang here for fifty, sixty, maybe even a hundred years, so our stories will sleep on the walls for the rest of this century, or at least until Cassie is an old woman and what happened in Iraq is a line in a history book, nothing more.

There's only a little space left before my words hit the edge of the wall and drop toward the floor. You who have found this will need to stoop to read the rest. But there's so much left to confess, here in these last few inches where I can still confess anything. I stole paperclips from my teacher's desk when I was seven and hid them in my closet in a silver horde. I hated saying prayers when I was little and by eleven decided there was no God. I resented Jeannie when she was born, how she stole my mother's attention. I gave a girl named Judy Popp a quarter to be my friend. The two of us took ribbons from the fabric store and once I stole buttons entirely on my own. I smoked a cigarette behind Munten's supermarket when I was twelve. I was boy crazy in school, a terrible flirt. I cheated on a history test in seventh grade. I necked with Zack Reese on our living room sofa when I was supposed to be babysitting. I smoked pot when I was a sophomore, hardly ever did homework. I waitressed in summers and never reported tips on my taxes. Dan on our honeymoon made love to me behind the wall in Washington in the middle of the day. For many years I drove without my seatbelt fastened. I always tell Dan I'm voting for one candidate, then go into the booth and vote for the other. As a young mother I was a failure at breast feeding. Five years ago at a convention in Phoenix I danced with a handsome teacher from Pennsylvania and let him tug me back to his room. I don't read as much as I should. I color my hair to hide the gray. I'm ten pounds overweight. My daughter is a torturer.

That's what you should know about me when it comes to truth. As for this country, our world, these times that to you will seem ancient. It's not much different than it's ever been. For the lucky ones, ease and prosperity. For the rest, war, nothing but war, nothing ever but war, war all the time now, war only war.